5-MINUTE

MARVEL

SPIDER-MAN

STORIES

MARVEL

Los Angeles
New York

"The Story of Spider-Man" adapted by Alexandra West. Illustrated by Simone Buonfantino. Based upon the Marvel comic book series *Spider-Man*.

"A Very Strange Night" adapted by Rachel Poloski. Illustrated by Roberto DiSalvo. Based upon the Marvel comic book series *Spider-Man*.

"The Widow's Sting" written by Jim McCann. Illustrated by Roberto DiSalvo. Based upon the Marvel comic book series *Spider-Man*.

"Mysterio's Revenge!" adapted by Alexandra West. Illustrated by Aurelio Mazzara and Gaetano Petrigno. Based upon the Marvel comic book series *Spider-Man*.

"Spider-MEN" written by Andy Schmidt. Illustrated by Aurelio Mazzara and Gaetano Petrigno. Based upon the Marvel comic book series *Spider-Man*.

"The Swashbuckling Spider" written by Arie Kaplan. Illustrated by Simone Buonfantino. Based upon the Marvel comic book series *Spider-Man*.

"Reptile Rampage!" adapted by Rachel Poloski. Illustrated by Aurelio Mazzara and Gaetano Petrigno. Based upon the Marvel comic book series *Spider-Man*.

"The Hunt for Black Panther" written by Jordan Lurie. Illustrated by Aurelio Mazzara and Gaetano Petrigno. Based upon the Marvel comic book series *Spider-Man*.

"Seeing Spots" written by Jim McCann. Illustrated by Simone Buonfantino. Based upon the Marvel comic book series *Spider-Man*.

"The Amazing Incredible Spider-Hulk" written by Arie Kaplan. Illustrated by Simone Buonfantino. Based upon the Marvel comic book series *Spider-Man*.

"Mega Meltdown" written by Jordan Lurie. Illustrated by Aurelio Mazzara and Gaetano Petrigno. Based upon the Marvel comic book series *Spider-Man*.

"Attack of the Portal Crashers" written by Calista Brill. Illustrated by Aurelio Mazzara and Gaetano Petrigno. Based upon the Marvel comic book series *Spider-Man*.

All stories painted by Tommaso Moscardin, Ekaterina Myshalova, and Davide Mastrolonardo.

For information address Marvel Press, 125 West End Avenue, New York, New York 10023.

Printed in the United States of America

First Edition, June 2017

Library of Congress Control Number: 2016944556

10 9 8 7 6 5 4

ISBN: 978-1-4847-8142-5

FAC-038091-19011

Storybook designed by David Roe

SUSTAINABLE FORESTRY INITIATIVE
Certified Sourcing
www.sfiprogram.org
SFI-00993
Logo Applies to Text Stock Only

MARVEL
marvelkids.com
© 2017 MARVEL

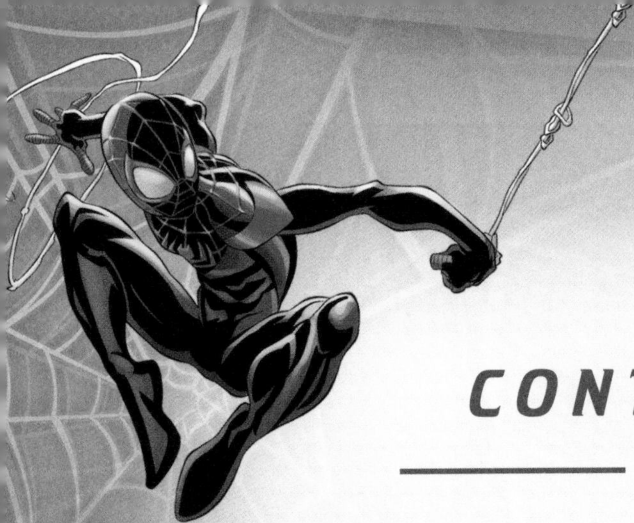

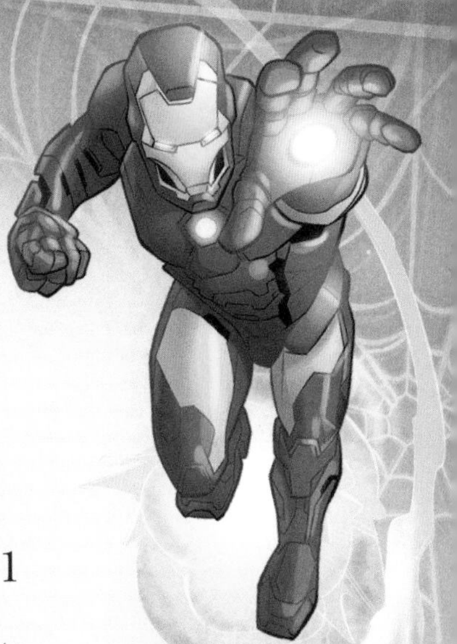

CONTENTS

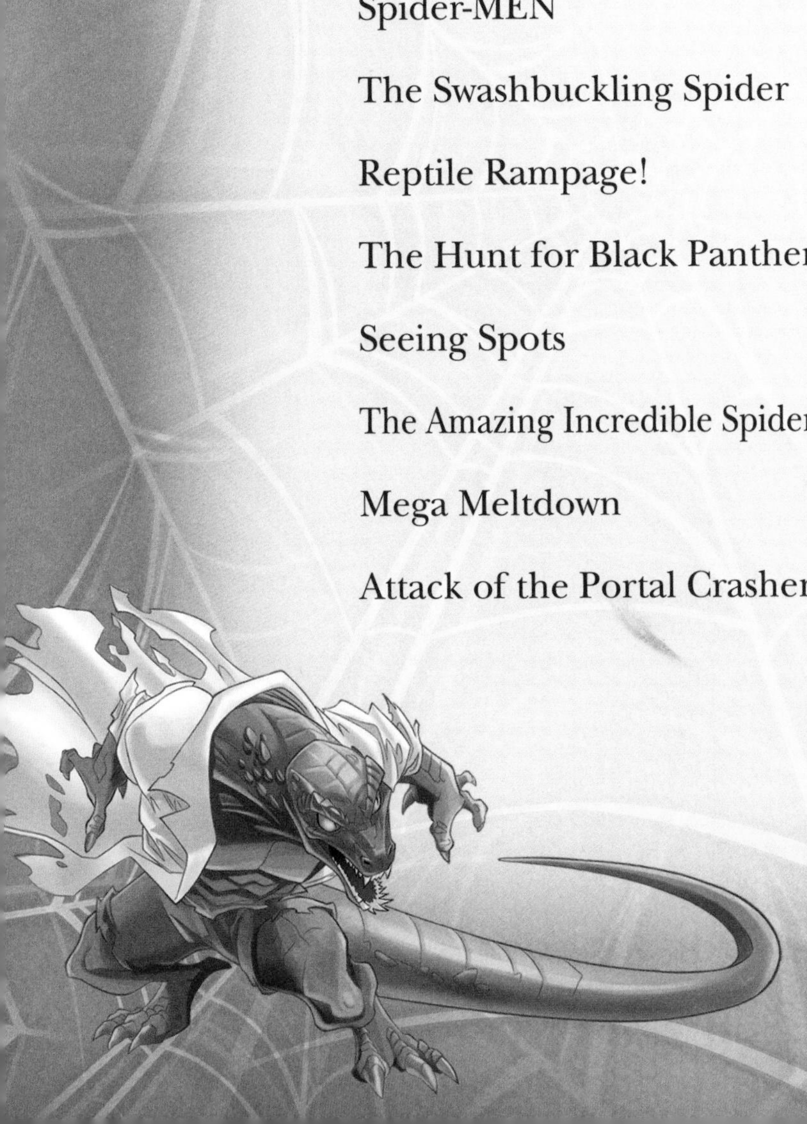

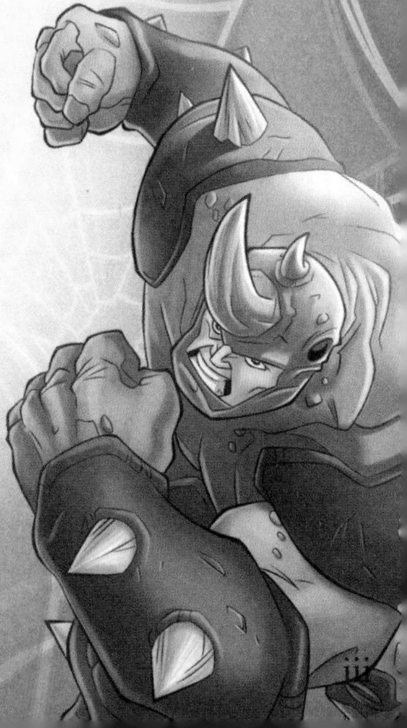

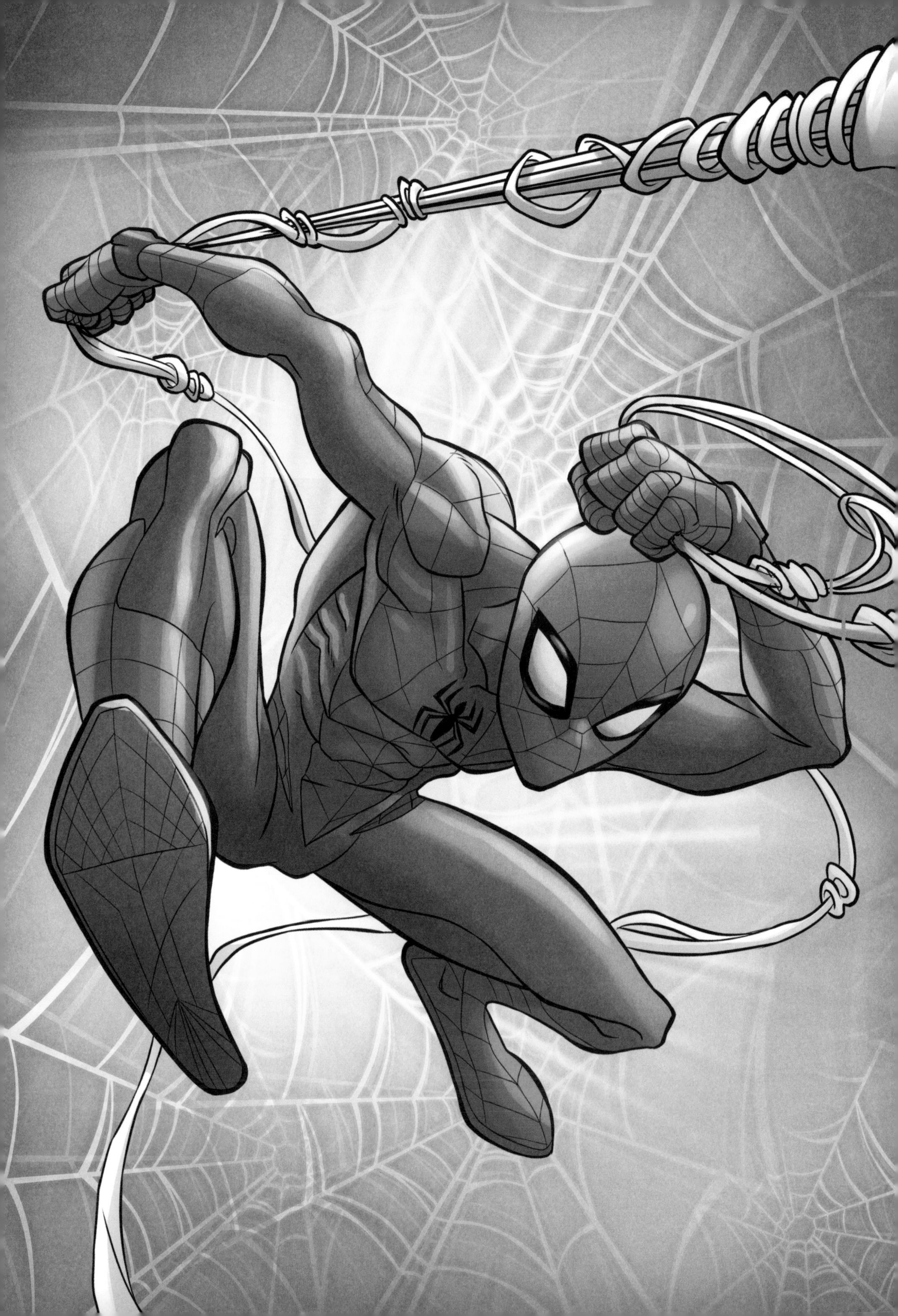

The Story of Spider-Man

Peter Parker was just your average teenager from Queens, New York. He lived with his Aunt May and Uncle Ben, and he attended Midtown High. Peter was very studious and was considered one of the smartest kids in school. Unfortunately, his good grades didn't make him very popular with some of his classmates.

Flash Thompson, the school bully, regularly tormented Peter. One day, Flash pushed him to the ground, and Peter's books and papers scattered everywhere. "Hey, Parker, you dropped your books," Flash sneered.

School was tough for Peter, but he was always happy at home. Aunt May and Uncle Ben loved Peter completely. Uncle Ben always reminded Peter that he was going to do something special with his life.

"You are incredibly smart, Peter," Aunt May said. "You have the ability to be anything you want to be."

"Well, actually, I was thinking that I might want to be a scientist someday," Peter replied.

Uncle Ben put his arm around Peter. "A scientist is a very important job. Science is power. And remember—with great power comes great responsibility."

Then one day Peter's life changed while he was on a school trip to the Science Hall. He was excited to see real-life scientists at work. But while Peter looked around at the exhibits, a spider passed through radioactive waves. Peter was so distracted, he didn't even notice the radioactive spider head right toward him.

At that moment, the radioactive spider bit Peter! He could never have imagined what an impact this one bite would have on his life. Peter Parker would never be the same.

Before Peter knew it, he had adopted many characteristics of a spider. He could cling to walls, he was superstrong, and he also had spider-sense. This meant that Peter experienced a strong tingling feeling that alerted him to danger. These skills made Peter extremely powerful.

Peter wanted to keep his identity a secret, so he stayed up all night creating a spider-suit and mask. He even stitched a large spider on the front of it.

Peter also worked hard to figure out how to control new powers. Using his vast knowledge of science, he made web-shooters and practiced shooting them in his bedroom. Peter's superstrong webs stuck to every surface. Soon his entire room was covered in webs!

Okay, so it's not as easy as it looks, Peter thought.

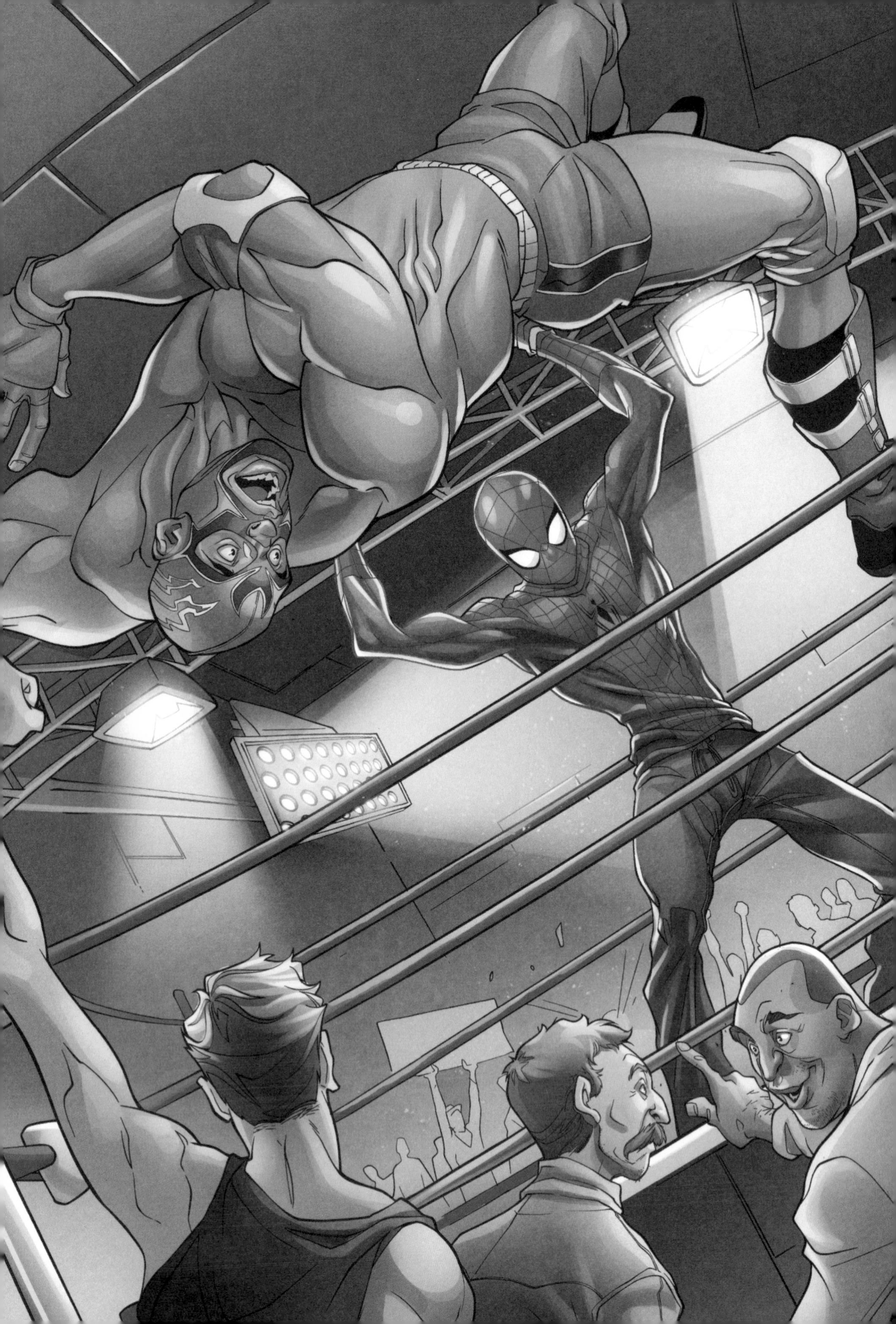

Like all teenagers, Peter wanted to make money. He needed a job where he could use his powers to his advantage. So Peter became a wrestler.

"Please welcome to the ring . . . Spider-Man!" the announcer would boom.

Peter used his powers to defeat every opponent. One night Peter noticed the wrestling gym was being robbed. Peter didn't care, and the robber ended up getting away.

When Peter got home later that night, he saw police cars in
front of his house. He raced inside and found out that someone
had attacked and hurt Uncle Ben. Aunt May and Peter were
devastated. The police officers told Peter not to worry because
they had the criminal cornered at an old warehouse. But Peter
knew he had to take matters into his own hands.

Peter put on his Spider-Man suit
and swung through the city. He was
determined to avenge Uncle Ben.

At last, Peter arrived at the warehouse. The thief was stunned as he watched Spider-Man in action. Spider-Man shot a web and trapped the crook. After getting a good look at him, Spider-Man realized that it was the same criminal he had watched escape from the wrestling gym.

If only I had stopped him then! he thought. Peter vowed that from then on he would help others whenever it was in his power. He would never let anything like this happen again!

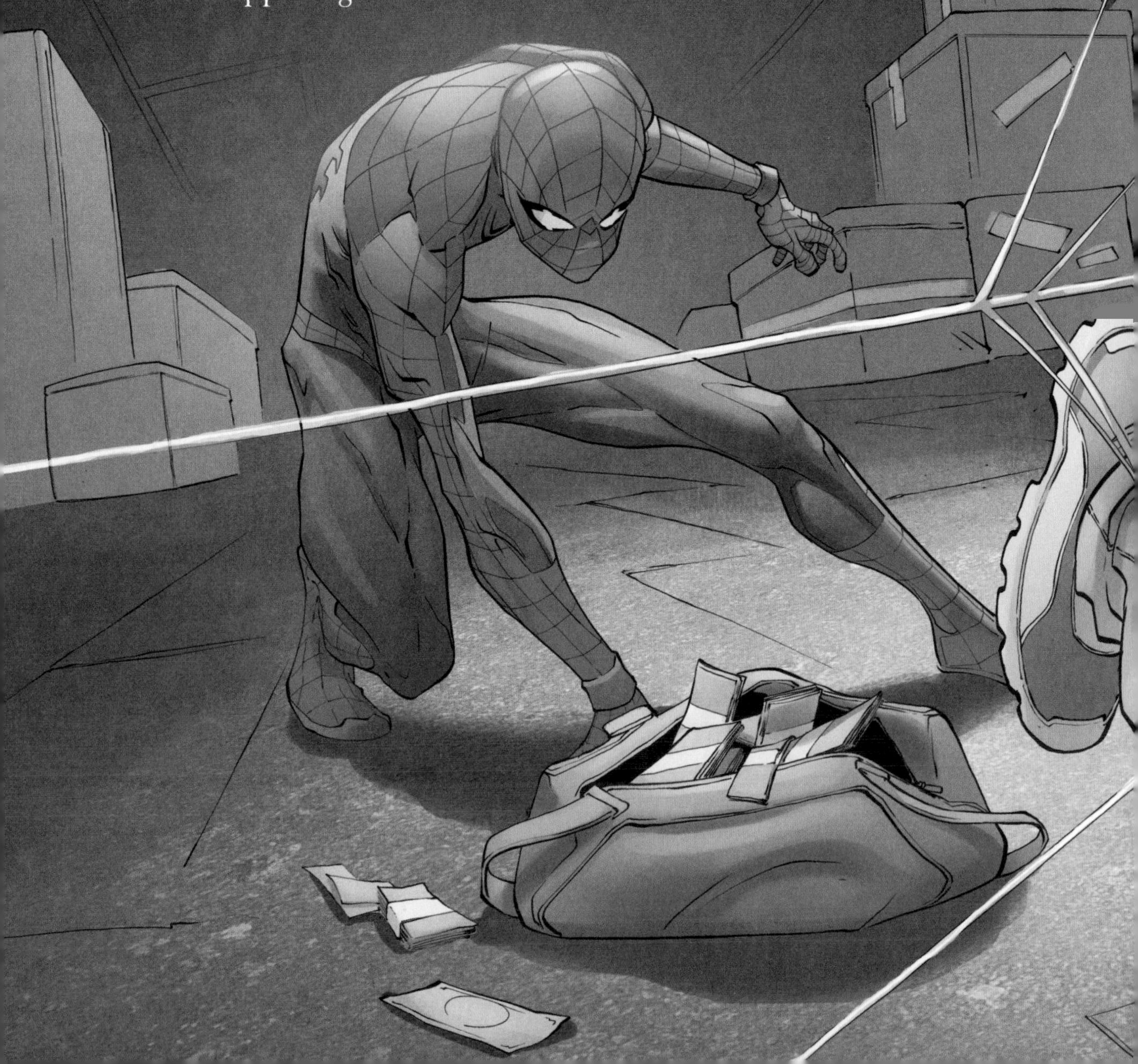

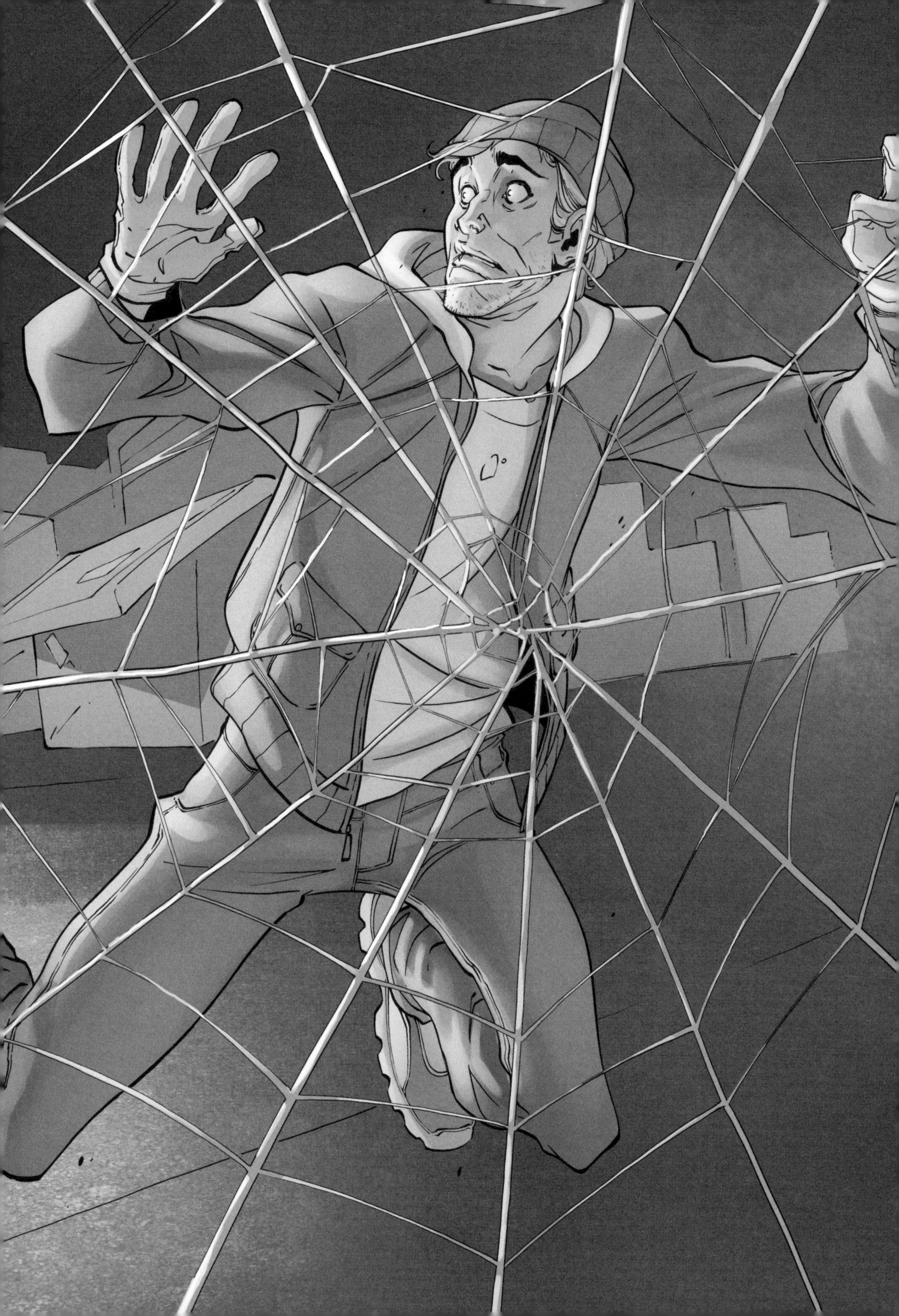

Just one month earlier, Peter would have been busy studying for his Chemistry final like any normal teenager, but everything had changed. He might still have to do homework from time to time, but Peter was also Spider-Man.

The next day at school, everyone couldn't stop talking about Spider-Man.

"I think he's great," Flash said as he looked at an article about the new hero. "He's just trying to help the city."

Peter smiled. If only Flash knew who Peter really was!

The next day, Spider-Man heard about another criminal on the loose in Manhattan. Spider-Man swung down to confront the villain, who he discovered had the ability to control electricity. It was Electro! The hero used his web-shooters, and after a few tries, the Super Villain was defeated.

In that moment, Spider-Man realized something. It was his destiny to always protect others, and if he worked hard enough, maybe one day he could become a great Super Hero. Spider-Man thought back to the words that Uncle Ben always used to say: *With great power comes great responsibility.*

Peter Parker might seem like your normal teenager, but there is a part of him that is extremely special. He is a Super Hero who can scale buildings and spin webs. He is the Amazing Spider-Man!

A Very
Strange Night

Spider-Man has been called many things: amazing, spectacular, and sensational. But today, no matter how hard Peter Parker tried, he wasn't feeling amazing, spectacular, or sensational. Today, Spider-Man was very, very sleepy. For the last week, Peter wasn't sleeping through the night. His dreams were troubling, silly, and sometimes downright spooky. A week of nightmares makes for one sleepy crime-fighter.

Peter didn't think much of it, until one very long spider-yawn almost allowed Shocker to ruin the Policeman's Ball! Spider-Man groggily swung into action. He webbed Shocker's gauntlets before knocking the vibrating villain to the floor with a well-timed kick.

"Look! Not only is he a menace, but Spider-Man was sleeping on the job!" J. Jonah Jameson shouted from his table as Spider-Man swung away.

Spidey knew he needed to see a specialist, someone who was truly an expert on dreams and the human mind. And he knew just the doctor to call. . . .

"Doctor Strange!" Peter said, greeting his old friend. "I'm sorry to interrupt, but I've been having trouble—"

"SLEEPING!" Doctor Strange said as Spider-Man entered the Sanctum Sanctorum. He had felt Peter's troubles long before Spider-Man had come to his doorstep. Doctor Strange threw his arms wide as he conjured the magical Eye of Agamotto. "The Eye of Agamotto has shown me that you've been experiencing nightmares," Strange told Peter. "And now it will show those nightmares to me."

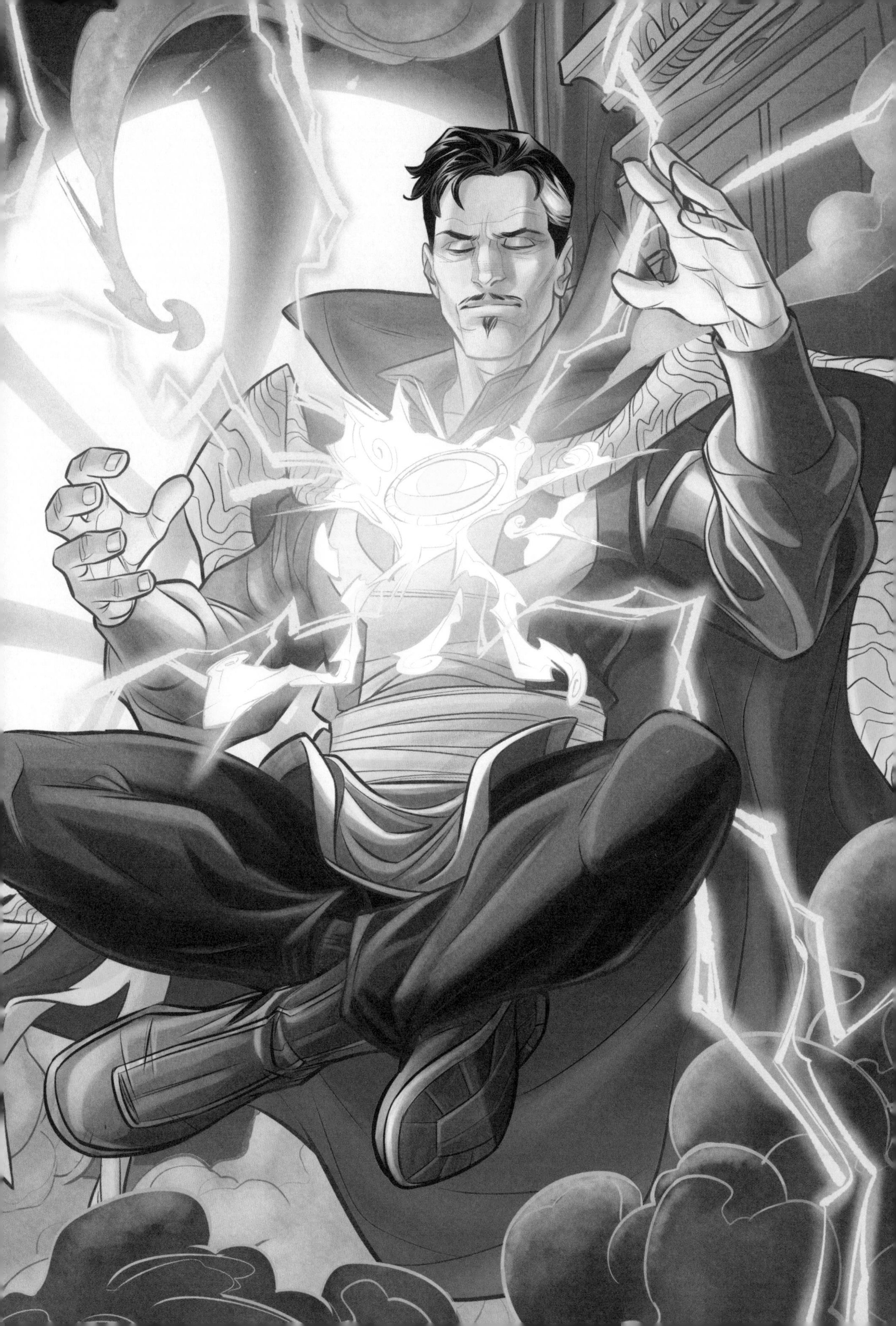

Soon, Doctor Strange was looking at Spider-Man's nightmares. In some, he was back in elementary school and forgot to wear his pants. In others, the Sinister Six were winning every battle against him. Doctor Strange was not only able to see the future and the past—he could also see right into a man's very soul.

"Your sleep is interrupted by the supernatural, your dreams are being invaded by the most dastardly of nocturnal threats—your mind is plagued by the villainous Nightmare himself!" Strange shouted.

With a snap of his fingers, Strange placed Peter into a deep trance. Then, with the help of the Eye of Agamotto, he dove straight into Peter's dreams.

Peter once again found himself pantsless in front of his entire class. And though he was embarrassed, he was no longer alone. Doctor Strange stood tall beside him, urging him to see the nightmare for what it truly was.

"The dream is yours to control," Strange told Peter.

Peter concentrated, and the class vanished. They were replaced by the master of bad dreams, Nightmare, and his trusty steed, Dreamstalker!

"The Sorcerer Supreme commands you to release your hold on this hero!" Strange shouted. But Nightmare simply laughed.

"I take power from dreams, Doctor Strange," Nightmare began, "and with a hero as strong as Spider-Man, I'll finally be great enough to defeat you!"

As Doctor Strange and Nightmare launched into combat, Peter knew he had to help the Sorcerer Supreme. Even in the dream state, Spider-Man had to lend a hand! And he realized he knew just how to do it—by using the power of imagination!

Peter thought and thought and thought, as hard as he could. To his amazement, the dream around him began to change! They weren't in Peter's school anymore but on a giant chessboard, and Spider-Man was in control of the pieces!

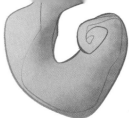

"It would seem Spider-Man is using the powers of his own dreams against you!" Doctor Strange declared to Nightmare.

Spidey played move after move, defeating Nightmare's pieces, until the villain was the only one left in play. Outnumbered, the villain retreated, leaving Peter's mind.

"You've won today, Strange, but you've not seen the last of me!" Nightmare shouted as he rode Dreamstalker out of Peter's mind and back to his home in the shadow realm.

"Don't worry, I look forward to defeating you again," Doctor Strange replied.

Peter woke with a start, pleased
to find the good Doctor waiting
with a warm cup of tea. "This is
Wong's special herbal blend,"
Doctor Strange said.
"It should calm
your mind after
a night like this."

After saying good-bye to his old friend, the tired hero swung home, changed into his pajamas, and slipped under the sheets. There were no monsters under the bed, and the only things in his closet were his clothes and his spider-suits.

So, for the first time in what felt like weeks, Peter Parker finally got an amazing night's sleep.

The Widow's Sting

Spider-Man was casually swinging through the streets of New York City. It was the weekend, and crime-fighting had been kind of quiet, not that he was complaining. Sometimes a Super Hero could use a nice day of just wall-crawling and web-slinging.

Looking down, he thought he saw a familiar face in the shadows. He swung over to take a closer look.

Landing on top of a building, he found himself face-to-face with the famous Avenger Black Widow!

"Hey, Widow! Making the rounds?" Spidey asked. "I'm having a slow day. How about you?"

At first, Black Widow looked surprised to see him, but then she smiled.

"I guess it is rather a light day, isn't it?" she agreed. Spider-Man noticed she was staring at something. He followed her gaze to Avengers Tower in the distance.

"If you're looking to head home soon, I could give you a ride," he offered. "Spidey-style."

Black Widow's smile widened. "Yes, it would be wonderful to see the Avengers again."

Again? Spidey thought. *Black Widow is an Avenger. Wouldn't she be there all the time?* But Spider-Man, not being an Avenger himself, shrugged it off.

Black Widow climbed onto Spider-Man's back. "Hold on," he said as they swung toward Avengers Tower.

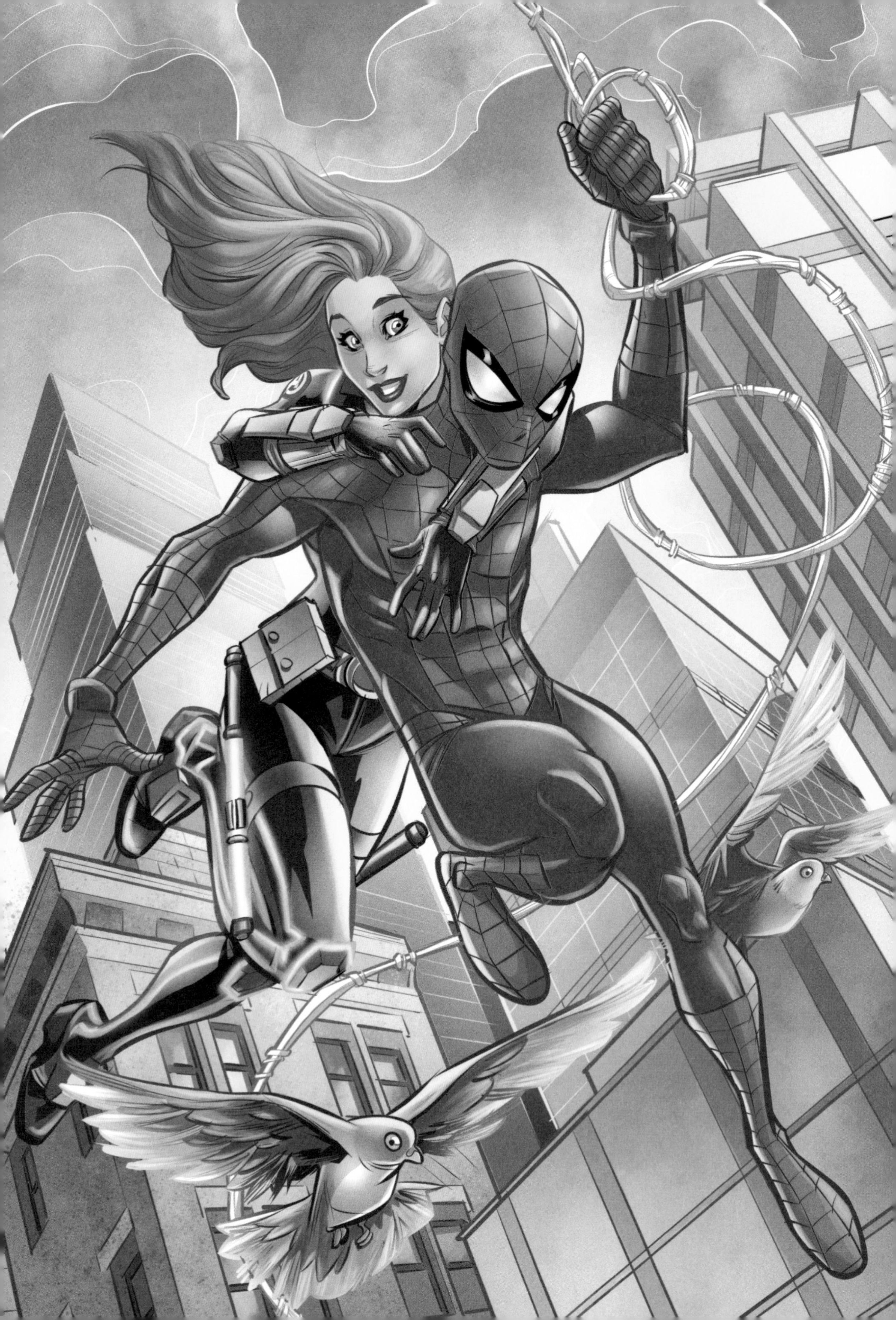

When they arrived at the tower, Spider-Man walked up to the security door and placed his hand on the scanner.

"Avengers Guest, Spider-Man. Identity: Confirmed. Welcome," the computerized voice said.

"What a friendly building," Spidey noted.

The doors opened, and Spider-Man began to walk inside.

Black Widow started to follow, but Spider-Man stopped her.

"Don't you have to check in?"

Black Widow lifted her cold eyes. Spider-Man's spider-sense tingled.

"Of course," Black Widow said, placing her hand on the security scanner.

The alarm began to sound. "Identity unknown. Intruder alert! Intruder alert!"

Black Widow, or whoever this imposter was, suddenly raised her arm and destroyed the scanner with her wrist blaster.

"Hey! That was a very friendly computer. You didn't have to blow it up like that, *Fake* Widow," Spider-Man said.

The Black Widow imposter lunged at Spider-Man. She was trying to get into Avengers Tower!

Spider-Man fired a web toward her, but the imposter vaulted through the air and landed gracefully on her feet behind him.

"Thanks for the ride, Spider-Man. You even held the door for me. Such a gentleman." Black Widow ran toward the open door—only to have it slam in her face!

"I guess you're not on the guest list," Spider-Man said.

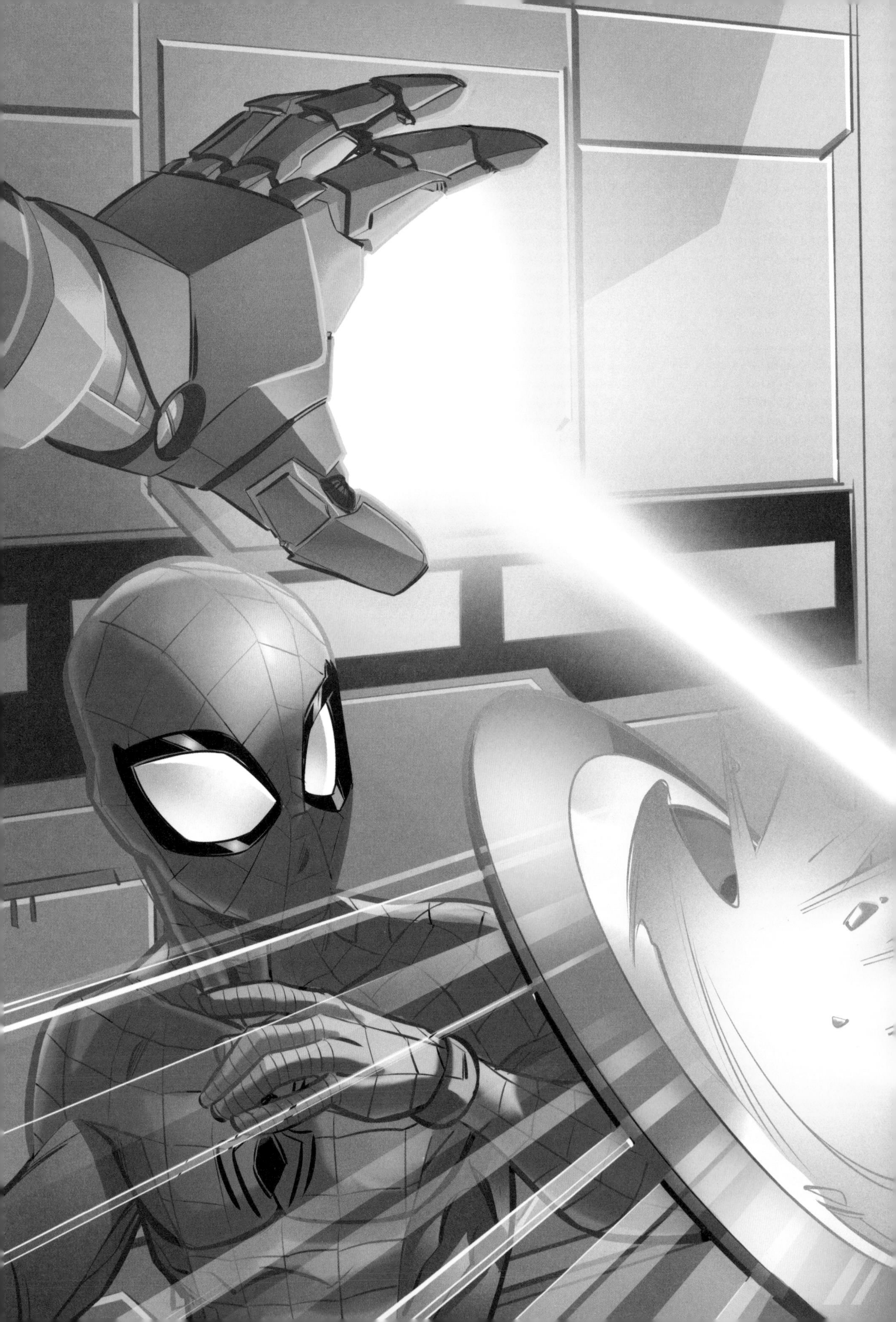

Frustrated, the false Black Widow blasted the doors. The doors still didn't budge.

"Keep knocking, I don't think they're going to let you in," Spider-Man said.

As Spider-Man and the imposter began to fight, a familiar-looking shield blocked one of the blasts that was about to hit Spider-Man. Another bolt of energy came shooting down from above, landing near the imposter's feet.

Looking up, Spider-Man saw two of
his Avengers friends coming to his aid:
Captain America and Iron Man!

"Boy, am I glad to see you guys!" Spidey said. "Oh, and even though it looks like it, that is NOT Black Widow!"

"We know," said Captain America. "The real Black Widow is away on a mission."

"That, and this Widow is trying to blast you," Iron Man said as he flew down to face whoever was impersonating their fellow Avenger.

The false Black Widow flipped and dodged Cap's shield as she fired her wrist blaster at Iron Man. "If only you had stepped aside and let me through, Spider-Fool."

"Sorry, rules are rules. I don't want to lose my guest pass," Spidey quipped, dodging one of the phony Widow's blasts.

Iron Man dove down, but the imposter was too fast, flipping over him and grabbing on to his back.

"You shouldn't give rides to strangers, Iron Man," the villain said.

Suddenly, Captain America's shield flew from behind and struck the imposter in the knees, knocking her to the ground with a thud.

Swinging into action, Spider-Man quickly webbed the evildoer's hands together, jamming the wrist blasters.

"I think it's time we find out who is behind the Black Widow mask," Spidey said.

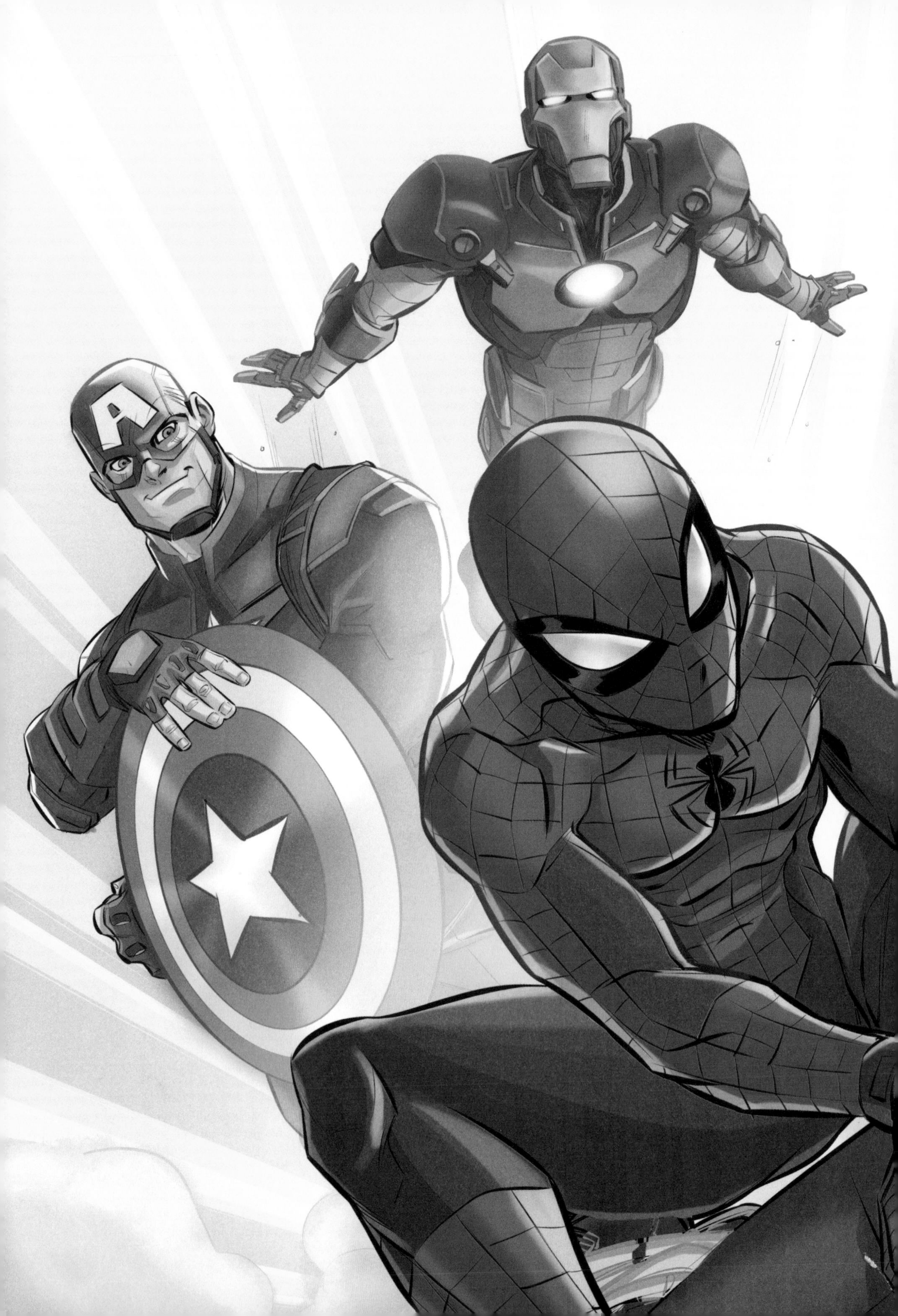

Spider-Man pulled on the imposter's hair, but instead of a wig coming off in his hands, the foe's entire body changed! Where Black Widow had been, there now lay the pale-faced villain . . . the Chameleon!

The Chameleon was a master of disguise, and his suit gave him the ability to take on the form of anyone.

"I thought Black Widow was looking a little pale today," Spidey said.

"And you nearly fell for it, too," the Chameleon snarled.

As Iron Man flew away with the Chameleon, Spider-Man turned to Captain America. "I hope this doesn't mean I'm banned from Avengers Tower for life."

Cap laughed. "Spider-Man, if you hadn't made sure that imposter followed the rules, the Chameleon would have been able to sneak in. You're always welcome here, son."

Spidey was relieved. "Good, can we go inside now? Avengers Tower has the best video games and snacks in town."

Mysterio's Revenge!

Thwip! Spider-Man shot a web across Fifth Avenue and swung past the Empire State Building. He was on his way toward the Daily Bugle. Peter Parker was late for work, and the only thing that could get him there in time was his web-shooters.

"Great," Peter said to himself as he fired another web. "If I'm late for work again, Mr. Jameson is going to explode!"

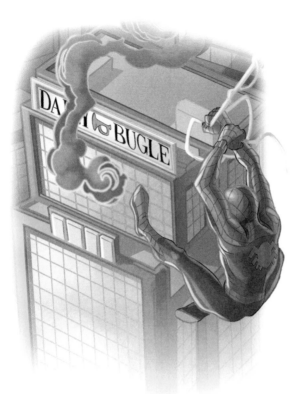

Just then, an explosion of green and purple smoke erupted from the top floor of the Daily Bugle building!

"Yikes! I didn't think he'd literally explode!" Spidey said. "Better get in there to see if anyone needs help."

Landing on the side of the building, Spider-Man crawled up the wall and looked through the window into the smoky office. That's when he heard a booming voice and his spider-sense started to tingle.

"Now that I have your attention," the bizarre voice began, "you will all witness the total destruction of the *Daily Bugle*!"

Spider-Man recognized that voice—it was his enemy Mysterio, the master of illusion! The menacing Mysterio was holding J. Jonah Jameson by the tie and addressing the terrified staff.

"No one can help you now, Jameson, not even Spider-Man!" the villain hissed.

"That's my cue!" Spidey said as he launched himself at the villain. Spider-Man caught Mysterio by surprise, and the two tumbled to the ground, locked in combat! As the Super Hero and Super Villain continued to fight, Jameson crawled to the exit. He jiggled the doorknob frantically, but all the doors had been locked from the outside.

They were trapped!

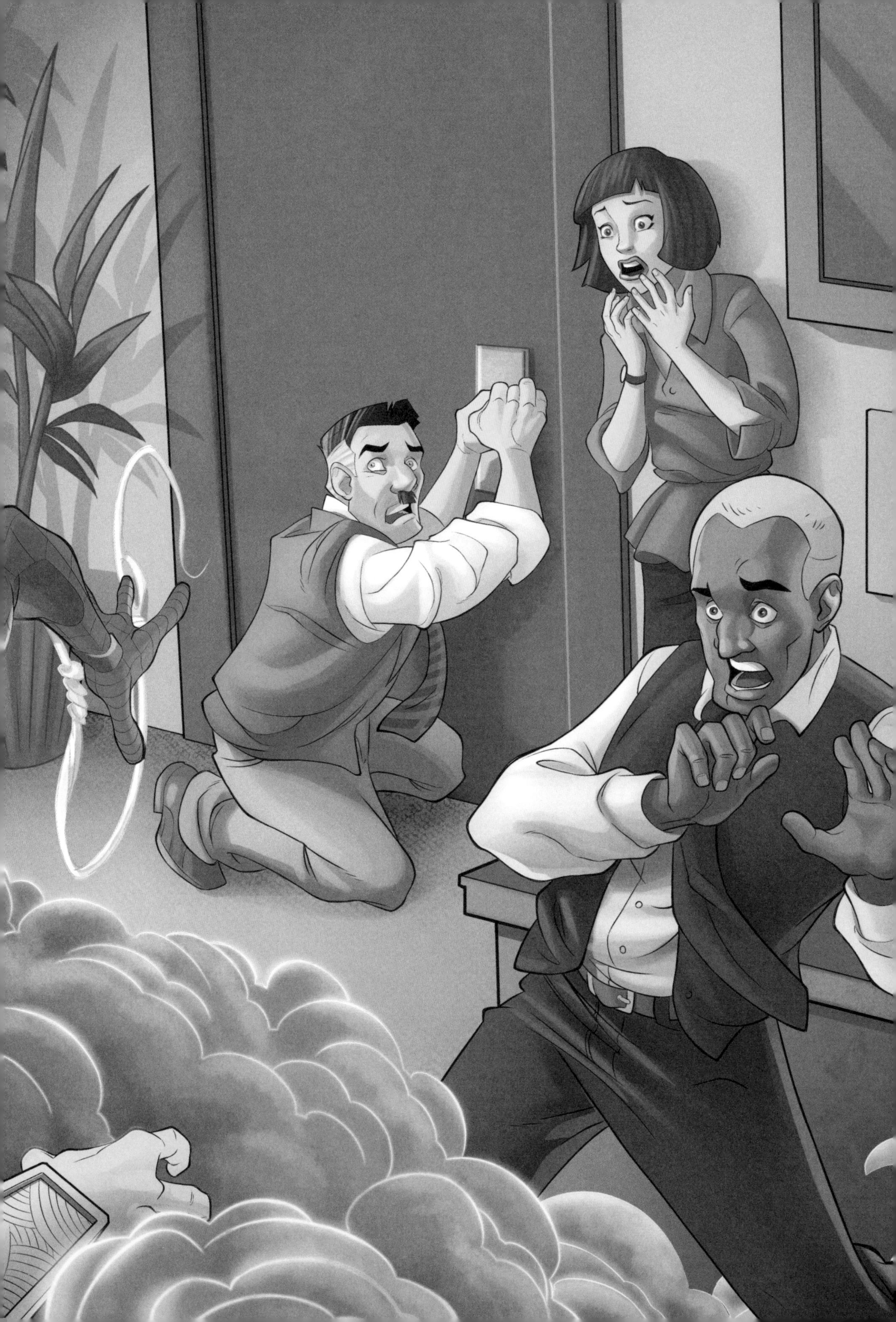

"The Amazing Spider-Man!" Mysterio began. "You're right on time . . . to meet your doom!" Mysterio raised his arms and the newsroom filled with thick green smoke. Then the villain disappeared into the fog right before everyone's eyes!

"Meet my doom?" Spider-Man said. "What do you suppose he meant by that?"

Mysterio's voice echoed eerily across the room. "Last I saw
you, J. Jonah Jameson, you promised that you could deliver
Spider-Man," the villain said. "Instead, I was defeated by
Spider-Man . . . and now, you will all pay!" With that, Mysterio
appeared through the smoke and lunged at J. Jonah Jameson.

Spider-Man knew he had to act fast! He fired a web and swung toward the villain. With unbelievable strength and speed, the amazing Spider-Man kicked Mysterio in the chest and then fired another web at Jameson, sticking him to the wall.

"Sorry to disappoint you, Mysterio, but I don't have plans to meet my doom for at least another sixty or seventy years!" Spidey said.

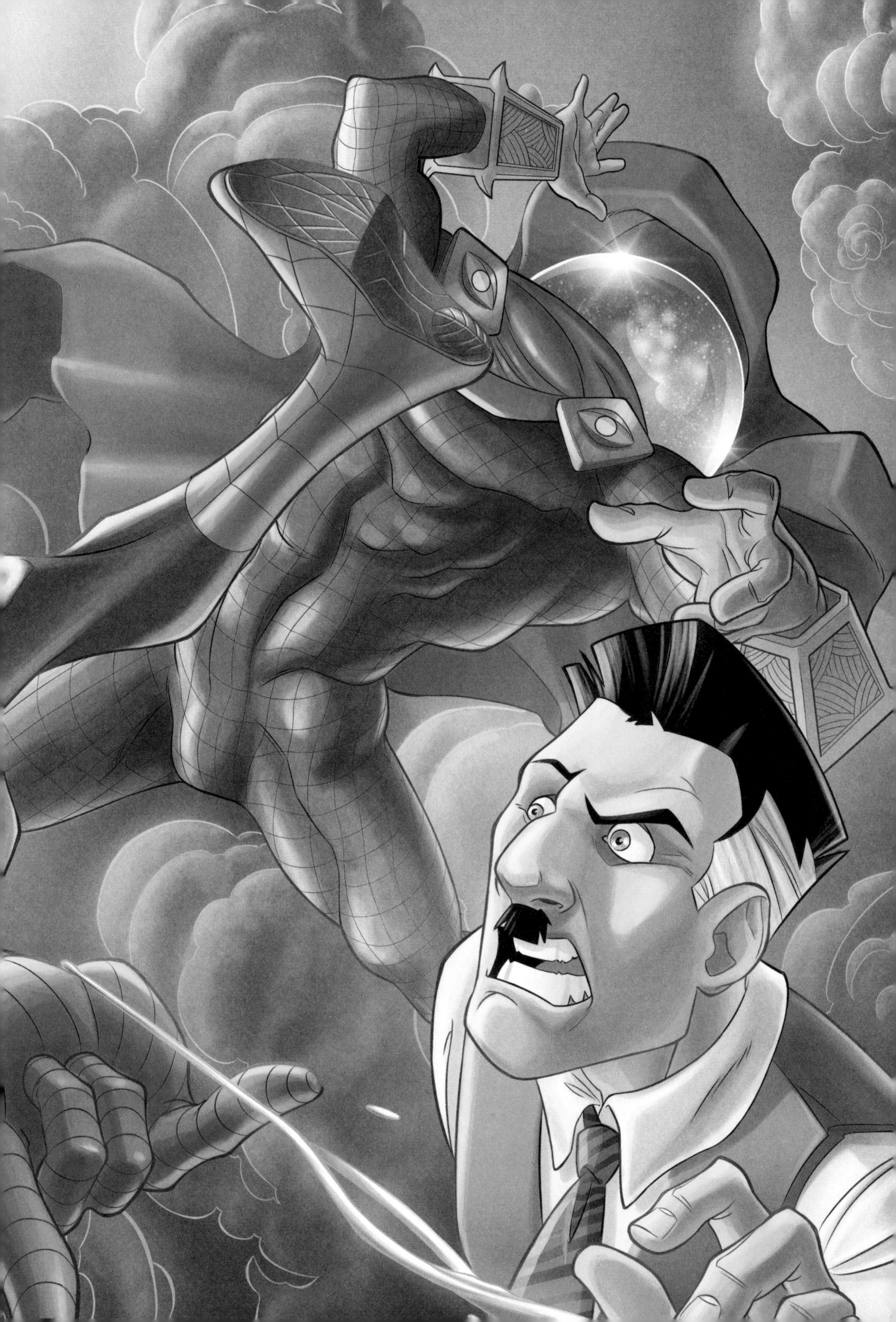

Spider-Man stood above the trapped Mysterio and removed the villain's glass helmet. But Spidey was shocked at the person he saw beneath the mask: it was Peter Parker!

"Parker!" Jameson yelled. "You're Mysterio?!"

Mysterio was a master of disguise, but only Spider-Man knew that the villain wasn't really Peter Parker. This must've been the disguise he was going to use in order to escape, Spidey thought. But how was Spider-Man going to save everyone in the *Daily Bugle* and prove that Mysterio wasn't Peter? While all these thoughts ran through Spidey's mind, the villain leaped forward and attacked!

Ow, I hit hard! Spidey thought. As he tried to pick himself up off the floor, Mysterio delivered another hard blow. *I can't believe I'm beating myself up!* Spider-Man was dazed, but he rolled across the smoky room. With Mysterio distracted by his precious helmet, Spidey looked around the office and realized the only person who wasn't there was the real Peter Parker. That's why Mysterio used him for his disguise! And that gave the wall-crawler an idea.

Spidey jumped across the room and crawled along the wall, completely hidden by the smoke. He grabbed a hoodie off a desk, zipped it up to cover his suit, and removed his mask. Now it looked like the real Peter Parker had shown up. "Hey, guys. Sorry I'm late."

Mysterio turned, enraged. "No! How did you get in?"

"*Two* Parkers?" Jameson said, confused. "Next there will be *two* Spider-Men!"

"Not if *I* have anything to say about it!" Mysterio said. The appearance of the real Peter Parker had worked. While everyone was distracted, Peter ducked beneath the smoke, put his mask back on, and charged at Mysterio.

Firing both web-shooters again and again, the Amazing Spider-Man captured Mysterio in a giant spiderweb for all to see. Then, with a CRASH, the police finally broke into the newsroom, just as Spider-Man jumped out the nearest window. "Here you go, boys," Spidey said to the cops as he swung away. "One gift-wrapped Super Villain, courtesy of you-know-who!"

A few minutes later, the real Peter Parker entered the newsroom. J. Jonah Jameson, who was still stuck to the side of the wall, looked down at him. "Parker," JJJ said, "you're late!" Peter sighed. It was just another day at the office for Peter Parker . . . and your friendly neighborhood Spider-Man!

Spider-MEN

You may have heard of Peter Parker, but do you know about the other Spider-Man, Miles Morales? Miles was just a young teenage boy when he gained spider-powers, made his own spider-costume, and called himself Spider-Man, too! Peter found Miles and the two became friends. Peter even began to train Miles to be a Super Hero.

So get ready, True Believer, to read a story with not one, but TWO Spider-Men!

Young Miles Morales and his friend Ganke were on a field trip with their school when they were caught by surprise. "Ganke, watch out!" Miles shouted to his best friend.

A flood of wild animals came stampeding toward them right in the heart of the Central Park Zoo!

Miles knew he had to help, but he couldn't put on his spider-suit. Ganke was the only one who knew about his powers. Putting on his suit would reveal Miles's secret identity!

"How did all these animals escape?" Ganke asked.

As if the universe was answering
his question, the Rhino charged out of
the woods and came barreling down
on Miles and Ganke. Ganke shouted at
Miles, "Jump, dude! He's
going to run you over!"

Luckily for Miles, the original Spider-Man snagged Rhino's horn just in time to save Miles from revealing his secret—and from a LOT of bruises.

"Yeehaw! You're worse than a bucking bronco, Rhino!" Spider-Man shouted.

When Miles realized that THE Spider-Man was there to help, he was thrilled.

Rhino jerked his head away, yanking Spidey off his back. WHAM! Spidey slammed down into the ground. "Ha!" Rhino bellowed. "Try and keep up, Spider-Man. My new animal friends and I are pretty wild."

As Peter lay on his back, Miles rushed over to see if he was okay. "Hey, Pe—uh, I mean, Spider-Man," Miles said. Peter was still a little woozy from hitting the ground.

"Miles! Great to see you, buddy. . . ." But before Peter could finish, he felt Rhino's hand grab his ankle.

Rhino flung Spidey through the air. As Peter whizzed by, he asked Miles, "How are your grades holding uuuuup!" Peter was tossed out of sight.

Miles stood face-to-face with Rhino, but he didn't budge. Not one inch. "No one scares animals and little kids when I'm around."

"You've got nerve, kid. I'll give you that," Rhino snorted. "You're lucky I got the web-head to finish, otherwise I'd give you the horn!"

The Rhino stormed off to find Peter Parker. He didn't realize that Miles was also a Spider-Man.

Miles looked left and right. All of his classmates, even Ganke, were gone! He remembered what Peter once told him: "With great power comes great responsibility."

Without another thought, Miles slipped on his mask and pulled on his suit.

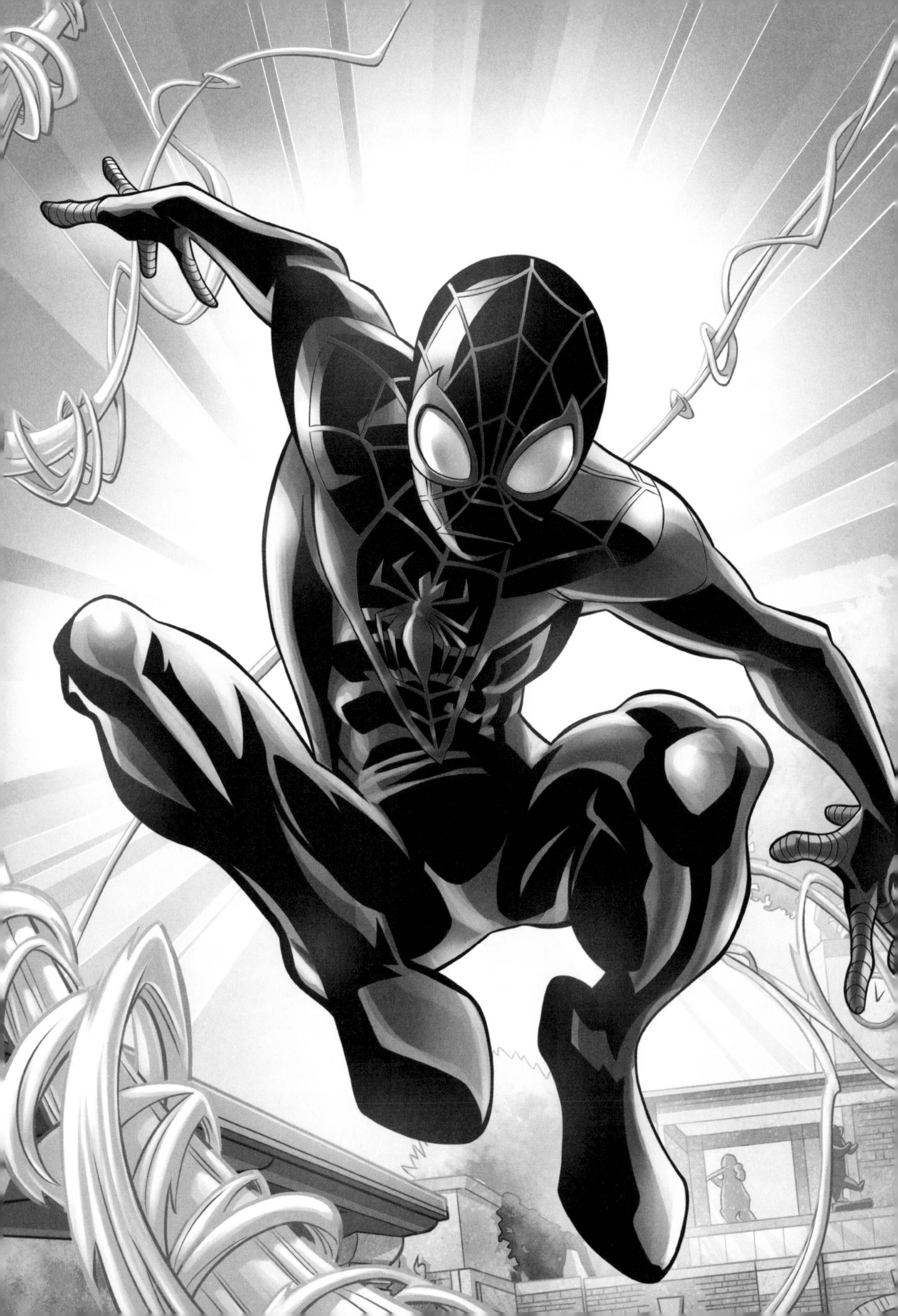

Where Miles once stood, now bounced the one and only (well, one of only two) Spider-Man! Miles's kick to Rhino's head was enough to give Peter a chance to get loose from the Super Villain's grip! "Thanks for the assist, Spider-Man," Peter said.

"How cute, the Spider-Men have come to meet their doom," Rhino snarled.

As Peter dodged Rhino's attacks, he called to Miles, "I need you to wrangle the zoo animals before they cause any more damage!"

Miles was hurt. "You don't want my help battling Rhino?"

Before Peter could respond, Rhino poked his horn right into Peter's behind—YOWZA!

Why does Peter not want my help? Miles thought to himself. *Maybe I'm not cut out for this whole Super Hero thing after all.* But just when Miles began to doubt himself, he remembered there was a job to do. It was his responsibility to wrangle the animals, and if that's what Peter needed, then that's exactly what he was going to do!

With great care, Miles wrestled a crocodile, webbing its mouth so it couldn't bite anyone. Using his wall-crawling ability, Miles climbed a large tree and guided a fluffy red panda to safety. Then, Miles contained a lion by electrifying the air using his venom strike—a spider-power that even Peter didn't have. Eventually, Miles helped all the animals find their habitats.

As Miles stood in front of the contained animals, he began to wonder where Peter and Rhino were.

"Ow. Ow. OW!" Suddenly Peter came bouncing across the pavement and slammed to a stop next to Miles.

"Rough landing," Peter joked. "Man, where's another Spider-Man when you need him?"

"Seriously, dude?" Miles asked.

Even though Miles was still learning his powers, Peter knew he was ready. "What do you say, Miles—you want to see if Rhino can beat the Spider-Men?"

Miles smiled. "I thought you'd never ask!"

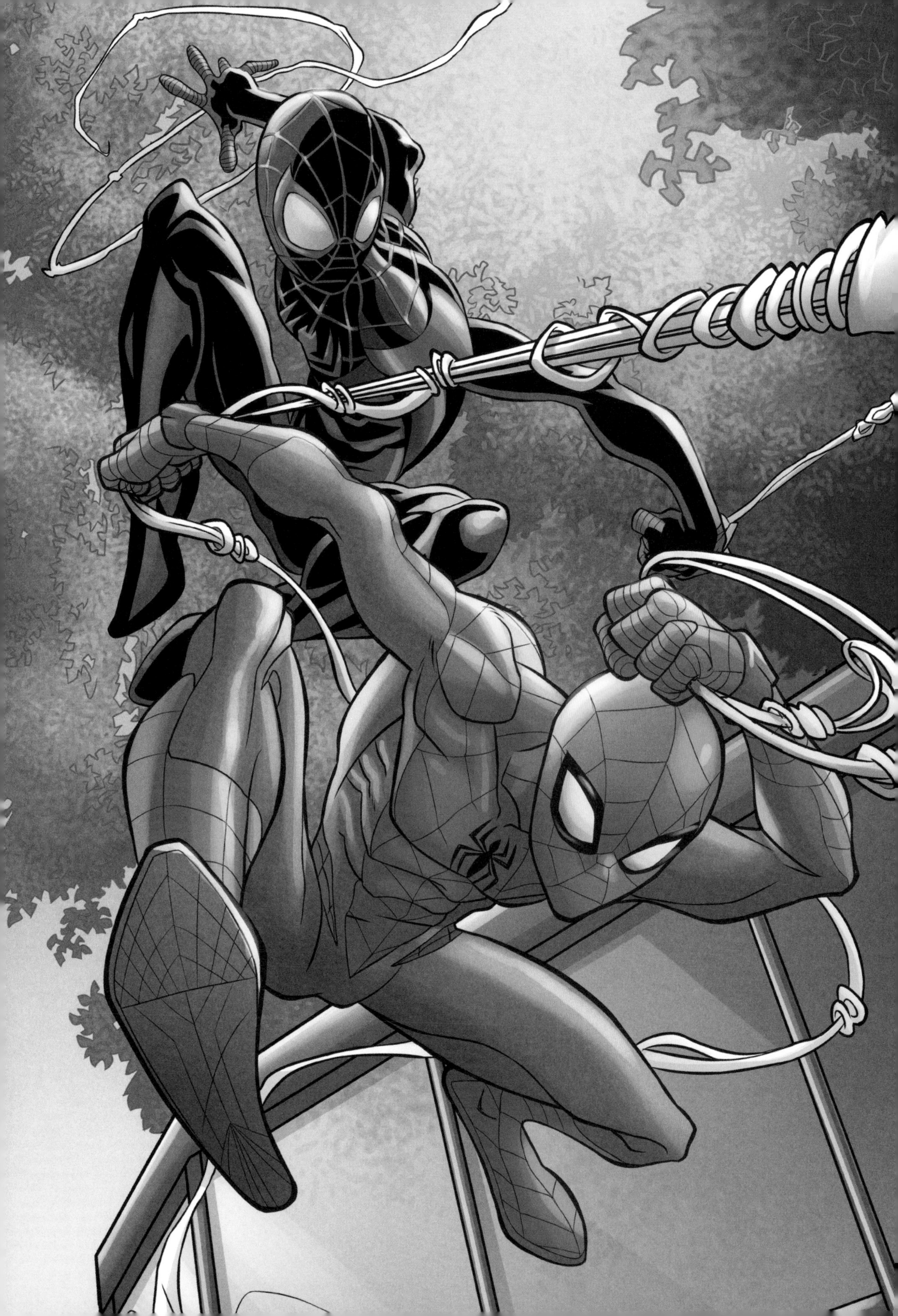

Together, the Spider-Men made the ultimate team.

"Have a nice trip!" Peter said as he webbed up the Rhino's feet.

"Man, your ugly mug is shocking!" Miles said as he used his venom strike to give Rhino an unexpected jolt.

"Oooh, nice one!" Peter cheered.

Rhino slammed into the pavement, knocking himself out cold. "Do you want to make the final wisecrack?" Peter asked.

Miles smiled. "How's this? Spider-Men: we put the NO in Rhino."

Peter burst into laughter and let out a theatrical sob. "My little baby is all grown up!"

After taking care of Rhino, the Spider-Men settled down for a well-deserved lunch break. "Remember when I told you that true heroes give back to their community?" Peter asked. Miles nodded as he took a loud sip of his soda.

"Well, giving the Central Park Zoo a dude dressed as a rhino wasn't exactly what I had in mind."

Miles grinned. "Still . . . he definitely fits in."

The Swashbuckling Spider

It was a good day to be Spider-Man. Earlier that morning, he had captured both Doctor Octopus and Sandman. Now, as the sun set, Spider-Man arrived at Avengers Tower. Nick Fury was there to greet him.

"Thanks for volunteering to keep an eye on the place while the Avengers are away," Nick said.

Spider-Man replied, with a firm handshake, "Not only will I keep one eye on the place, I'll keep two!"

Spider-Man secretly hoped
that if he did this favor for
the Avengers, they might let
him join their team someday.
Before Nick Fury left, he gave
Spider-Man one important
instruction: watch the
security monitors.

"Don't worry, I've got this,"
Spider-Man said confidently.

But watching the monitors
was dull. So Spider-Man
decided to do some exploring.
His first stop was Tony Stark's
lab. Inside, Spidey found
a scroll that looked like a
pirate's treasure map. But the
scroll was covered in strange
symbols. A note below the
scroll read, "HANDS OFF!"

Spidey knew he shouldn't touch the map. The last time he fiddled around with mysterious artifacts in Tony's lab, he got sent back in time to the Old West. But his curiosity got the better of him! He held the map up to the light and saw glistening circuitry and bizarre icons woven throughout the parchment.

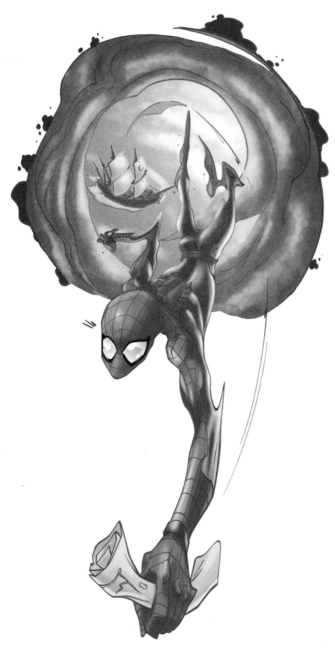

Without thinking, Spider-Man
tapped one of the icons. An
enormous portal opened up—
and sucked the web-slinger right
into it.

"Whoaaa! Not again!" Spidey
shouted as he plunged deeper
down the portal.

Dazed, Spidey realized he was being tied up by a huge, hairy man. The man grabbed the wall-crawler, yanking him forward. " 'Tis a masked scurvy dog who appeared out o' nowhere, sir!" the man growled. A massive buccaneer with a braided beard turned to look at Spider-Man. It was Blackbeard the pirate!

"Oh, hello, Blackbeard, the most notorious pirate who ever lived," Spider-Man quipped. "I would love to stay and chat, but I better get going." Spider-Man attempted to flee, but the legendary pirate was not going to let Spider-Man go so easily.

Blackbeard eyed the map in Spidey's pocket. Thinking it was a treasure map, the pirate king snatched it. Then he shoved Spider-Man onto a wooden plank that jutted out over the waves. The web-slinger bumped into a man with a hook for a hand, who was already standing at the edge of the plank. "I guess we're plankmates," Spidey joked to the man, who spun around to face him. It was Nick Fury!

"Nick!" Spider-Man said, shocked.

"Who's Nick?" the man replied. Spider-Man realized that this wasn't actually Nick Fury. Nick had once told Spider-Man a story about his ancestor. "You're 'One-Eyed' Fury!" Spider-Man said. "You're that English spy. Man, I thought Nick was pulling my leg."

"Will you keep your voice down, sir!" One-Eyed Fury said in a loud whisper. "I'm undercover."

"How's that working out for you so far?" Spidey asked.

But before they could chat any further, Blackbeard knocked Fury and Spidey overboard!

Thinking quickly, Spidey used his super-strength to break through his bonds. Then he shot his webs and swung over the water, catching Fury in midair. Both of them were now safely on deck . . . or so they thought. Spider-Man was untying Fury's ropes when Blackbeard's crew charged at them.

"Don't worry, I've got this." Spidey smirked, swiping Fury's hat. "Oh, and may I? I love a good costume!"

Spider-Man covered the attacking
pirates with a net of webbing. Then he
tossed the webbed swashbucklers at the
remaining pirates, making them scatter
like billiard balls.

"Eight ball in the corner pirate!"

Suddenly, Blackbeard snapped his fingers, and two ferocious female buccaneers appeared. "Ahoy, scallywags! May I introduce ye to me buckos Sandy Dunes 'n' Doctor Squidlegs," Blackbeard boomed. "Ladies, attack!"

Spidey turned to One-Eyed Fury. "I can't understand a word this guy says."

Doctor Squidlegs's mechanical tentacles hissed and clicked as they came down all around Spider-Man and One-Eyed Fury, while Sandy Dunes whipped up a huge sandstorm. But Spider-Man and One-Eyed Fury were ready! The two heroes worked together as a team to take on the villains.

"Follow my lead, Fury!" Spider-Man shouted as he covered Doctor Squidlegs in webs.

"Is that all you got?" One-Eyed Fury asked. "Watch this!" The spy pressed a button on his sleeve, and his hook hand transformed into a water cannon. A jet of water sprayed out of the cannon, melting Sandy Dunes!

Suddenly, the deck began to shake. Blackbeard had used the map to open a portal! Thinking quickly, One-Eyed Fury used his water cannon to pummel the famous pirate and his comrades, knocking them out cold.

"Not bad for a guy with one eye . . . and one hand," Spider-Man said as he grabbed the map and jumped through the portal.

"Thank you, sir!" One-Eyed Fury called out as he took control of the ship. "I hope we meet again!" As Spider-Man entered the portal, he could've sworn he saw something else fly through the portal with him.

The portal dropped Spider-Man back in the twenty-first century. *That was so much fun! Way more fun than watching monitors— Oh no! The monitors!* Spidey rushed back to make sure nothing bad had happened while he was gone. Everything looked quiet enough, except for a flash of movement on one screen. It was Blackbeard's parrot, and Spider-Man had to catch the feathered felon before it wrecked all the furniture in Avengers Tower.

Reptile Rampage!

Dr. Curtis Connors, also known as the Lizard, was in trouble. Peter Parker knew it as soon as he saw all the pictures of the Lizard splashed across the front page of the *Daily Bugle*. Peter also knew that his boss, J. Jonah Jameson, would be mad that Peter hadn't delivered exclusive pictures of the Lizard.

As soon as Peter walked into the *Daily Bugle*, J. Jonah Jameson called him into his office.

"Parker, the Lizard is on the loose, and I need pictures," he demanded. "I don't care if you have to camp out in a swamp. I want a shot for the front page. And I also want a picture of Spider-Man fighting the Lizard," JJJ shouted. He always expected perfection.

"I'm your man. I'll get you those shots," Peter told his boss.

Meanwhile, Dr. Connors's wife, Martha, was very upset. She noticed her husband mixing up a strange formula earlier that week. She knew that he was trying to create a serum that would help him grow back his missing arm, but she also knew that it came with a serious side effect. It turned Dr. Connors into an evil villain called the Lizard!

Spider-Man found Martha
Connors sitting on her porch. She
was looking at a picture of her husband.

"I wish he didn't care about growing
back that arm." She looked at Spider-Man
with concern.

"I'll find him," Spidey told her. "Don't worry."

"Please hurry," Mrs. Connors said. "You need to
bring him to the lab and feed him the antidote."

"Got it! He won't be a lawless lizard much longer.
Soon he will be back to being good old Dr. Connors."

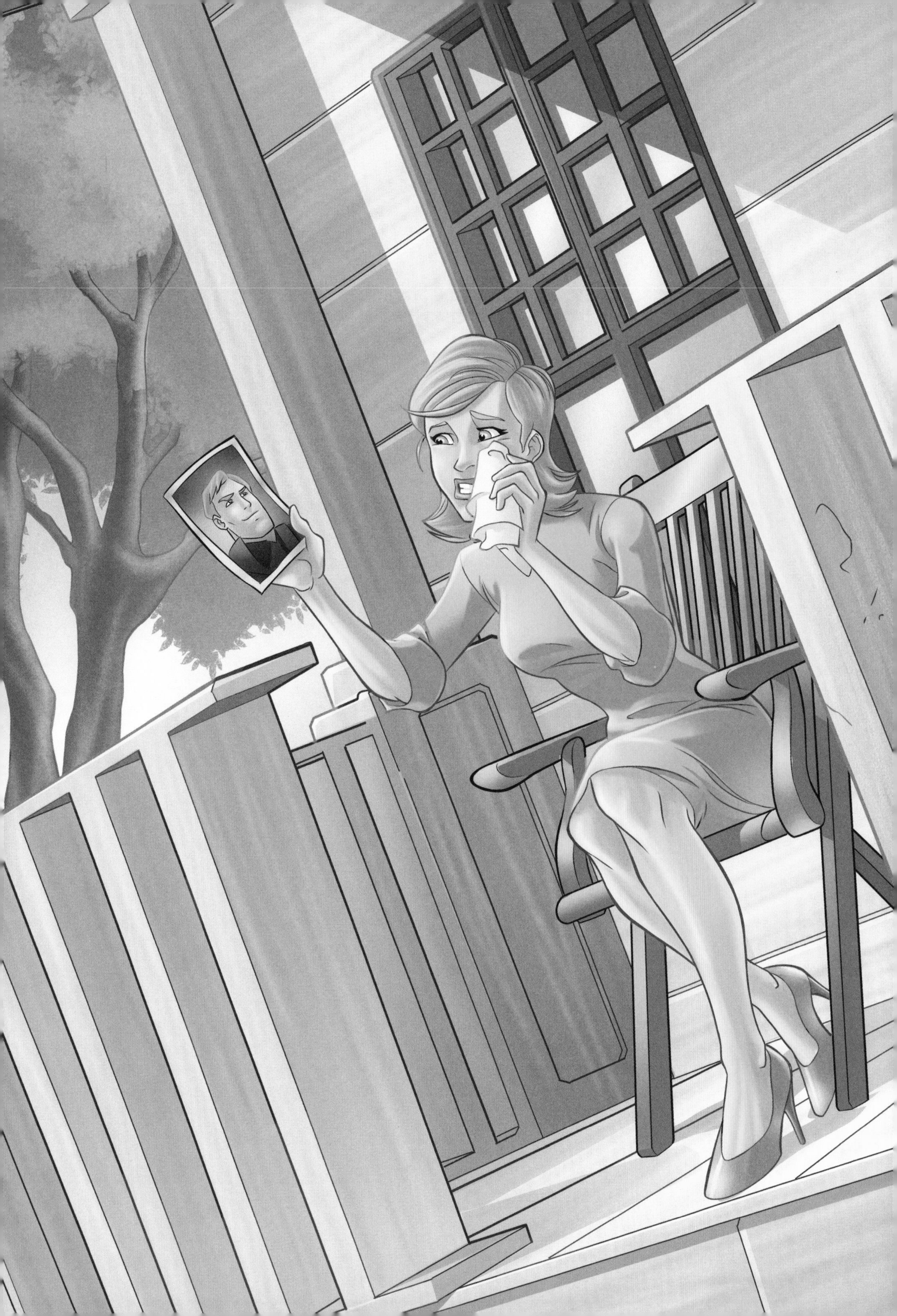

Spidey searched New York City
up and down. Finally, he spotted
the Lizard. Spider-Man chased him into
an ice cream shop, hoping to lock the cold-blooded
beast in a freezer, which would diminish the Lizard's strength.
Unfortunately for Peter, the Lizard escaped!

"I'm not a fan of frozen treatsss," the Lizard called out to Spidey.

"If you try to run from me, you're going to be on a *rocky road*," Spidey taunted.

The Lizard stomped through the streets, creating a wave of destruction, crushing car windows and damaging storefronts.

Spidey trailed behind the Lizard as
they made their way up the building
where Dr. Connors kept his lab.

"Once you go in there, I can promise
you you're not coming out," Spidey said
as he scaled the side of the building. The
Lizard tried to knock Spidey down with
his powerful tail, but it didn't work.
The Lizard roared, and it echoed
through the city. People came out
from the surrounding buildings
and crowded around to see
the excitement. Spider-Man
was going to save the day!

Spider-Man found a
window to climb through
and made his way into
the lab, grabbing the antidote. Suddenly, the Lizard crashed
through the door, followed by a group of angry reptiles. The
Lizard had given them something that let him completely
control their minds. They were ready to attack! Spider-Man
looked to his left and saw a giant snake slithering toward him.

"Yikes!" Spider-Man shouted as the monstrous snake coiled itself around his leg. Spidey quickly fired webs at the Lizard as more and more reptiles attacked.

The Lizard dodged Spider-Man's webs and swung his enormous tail. Spidey flew through the air, crashing straight into the lab table. But Spider-Man kept firing his webs! He didn't know if he was going to be able to fight both the Lizard and the cold-blooded fiends.

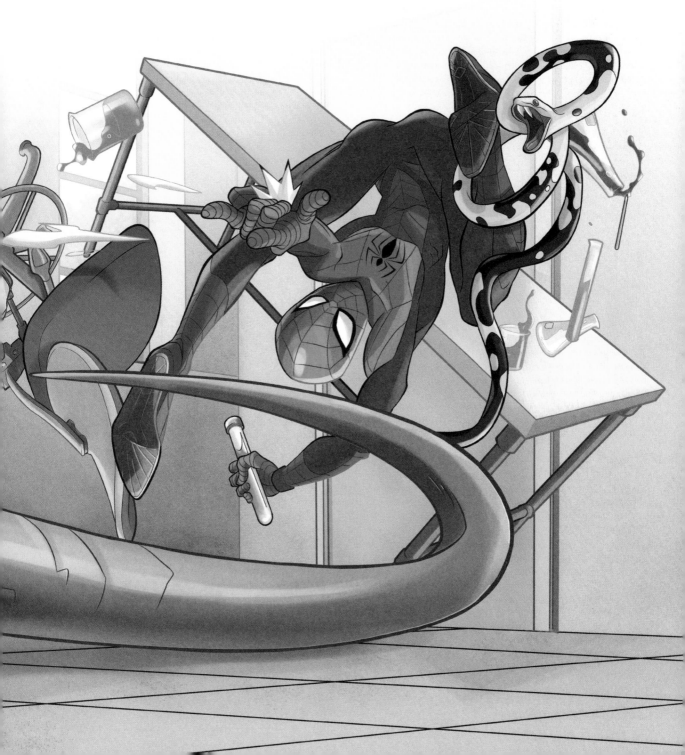

Spider-Man was in full battle mode with the reptiles when the Lizard threw a desk at him.

"Whoa, bad lizard!" Spidey called out. "Dr. Connors, do you realize what you are doing? You have to stop the Lizard!" But it was pointless. Dr. Connors had no control once the Lizard was unleashed. There was no use reasoning with a monster.

In between fighting, Spidey eyed the antidote. The
Lizard used the opportunity to unleash his final attack.
He ordered the reptiles to hold Spidey down as he began
to strike him over and over. Spider-Man fought back
hard, making sure not to bump into the antidote.
Finally Spidey broke free, grabbed the antidote,
and poured it into the Lizard's open jaws.

Within seconds, the Lizard began to
morph until he slowly became Dr. Connors
again. Spider-Man was relieved to see the
doctor's familiar face.

"Wow, what happened?" Dr. Connors
asked.

"It's a long story." Spidey sighed.

Soon Martha Connors had her husband
back, and J. Jonah Jameson had his front-page
spread. Everyone was happy!

That night, Peter came home to one of Aunt May's amazing home-cooked meals.

"How was your day, Peter?" Aunt May asked. Peter didn't even know where to begin. Aunt May didn't know Peter was Spider-Man, and he certainly couldn't tell her about his fight with the Lizard. "Don't forget to save room for dessert, Peter," Aunt May said as Peter finished his dinner. "I picked up a pint of ice cream. Your favorite, rocky road."

ROCKY ROAD

The Hunt for Black Panther

Kraven the Hunter loved to hunt wild animals. The only thing he loved more than hunting was the fame that came along with it. But one day, after Kraven had captured a pair of cheetahs, he didn't feel the same sense of accomplishment he normally felt after a successful hunt.

Kraven hungered for a new prey that would give him a real challenge. But where could he find such a foe?

A few days later, Peter Parker was sent by the *Daily Bugle* to photograph the annual Protection of Endangered Animals conference in Upper Manhattan. Giving the keynote speech was none other than T'Challa, ruler of the African nation of Wakanda.

Peter was excited for the chance to actually see T'Challa speak. The king was a compassionate ruler and a scientific genius.

But T'Challa had a secret. He was also the Super Hero Black Panther!

"In order to protect the animals of Earth," the king began, "it is our duty to fight back against illegal hunters and poachers."

Black Panther protected his nation and its animal kingdom from villains by using his superhuman strength, speed, and agility. One of those villains was Kraven the Hunter.

Craving a new challenge, Kraven knew that this conference was the perfect place to find his next prey—Black Panther! The villain burst through the window in a spray of broken glass.

"T'Challa!" he bellowed. "I request a meeting with the Black Panther."

T'Challa's eyes narrowed. "Black Panther will never bow to the likes of you!"

Kraven smirked. "I assumed there would be some protest."

"Which is why I brought some backup!" Kraven shouted. Just then, Kraven let out a high-pitched whistle, and two cheetahs leaped down from the window above! "No one here is allowed to leave until the Black Panther is mine!"

In the chaos, Peter Parker's spider-senses were tingling like crazy. Peter knew he had to act fast. This place was turning into a zoo!

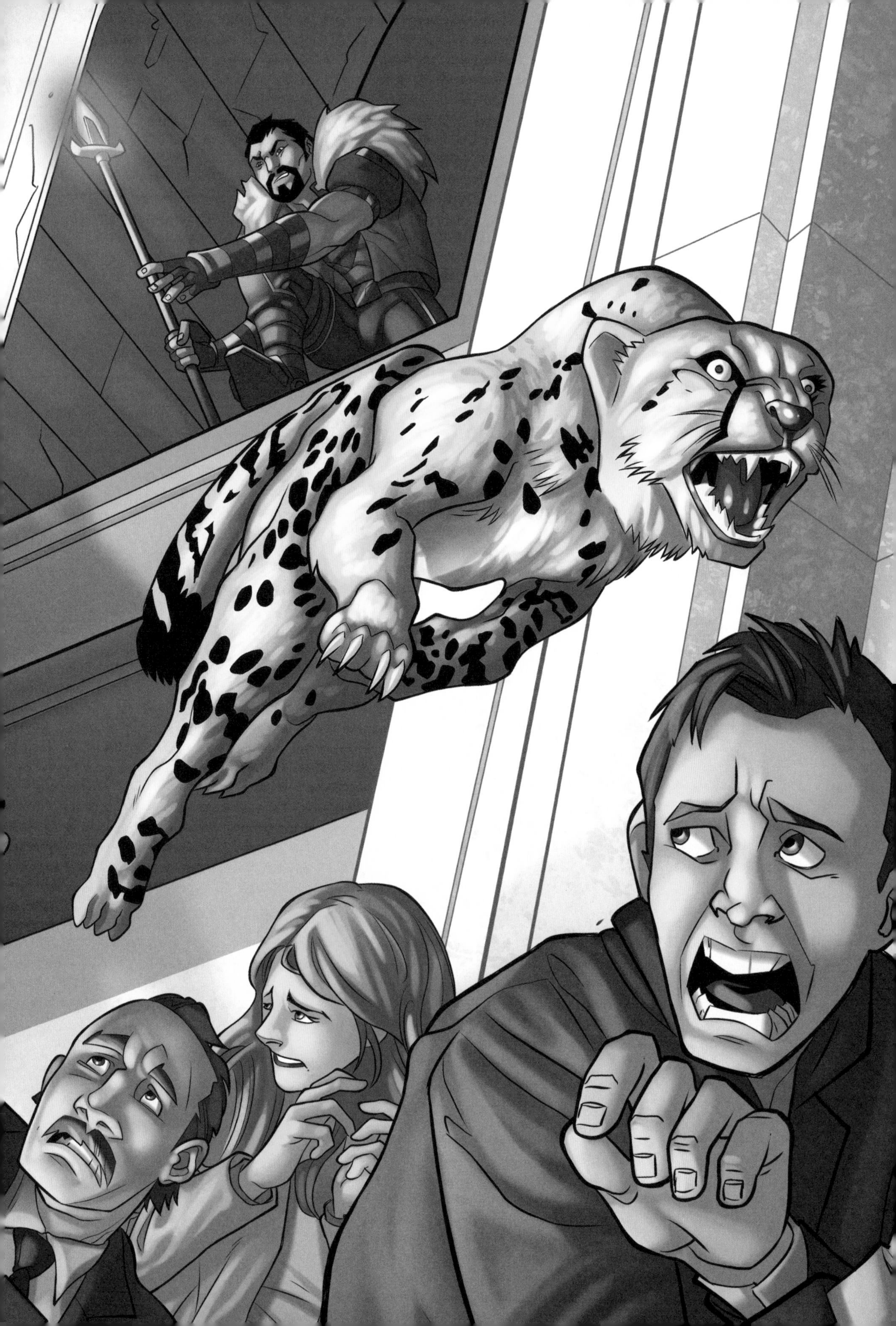

Meanwhile, T'Challa's bodyguards, the Dora Milaje, attempted to move the Wakandan king to safety.

"Save your energy," he commanded. "It's time for Black Panther to strike."

Black Panther turned around to discover he had been joined
by Spider-Man!

"What are you doing here?" Black Panther asked.

"Nice to see you, too," Spider-Man said as he fired a ball of
web fluid at the nearest cheetah. "Stand back—I've beaten
Kraven before. I can deal with these overgrown house cats."

"Spider-Man, no! You must be careful!" Black Panther tried to
warn the web-slinger, but it was already too late.

"Whoa! Nice kitty!" Spider-Man exclaimed as the cheetah grabbed his web and lunged toward him.

Acting fast, Black Panther grabbed the cheetah before Spider-Man was harmed. "Listen to me. My animal instincts tell me that these creatures are being held here against their will. They will only attack you if they are provoked."

But Spidey wasn't out of danger yet! Kraven threw a spear at the web-slinger, but Spidey rolled out of the way just in time!

"I'll calm them down while you get Kraven," Black Panther said to Spidey.

"On it!" Spider-Man said as he swung toward the balcony.

While holding back the cheetahs, Black Panther massaged the backs of their heads. Kraven had found a way to increase the aggression of these animals. Luckily, Black Panther was more familiar with wildlife. He safely pressed down on the cheetahs' pressure points to relax the animals' anger.

"That should calm you down," he said, petting the cheetahs.

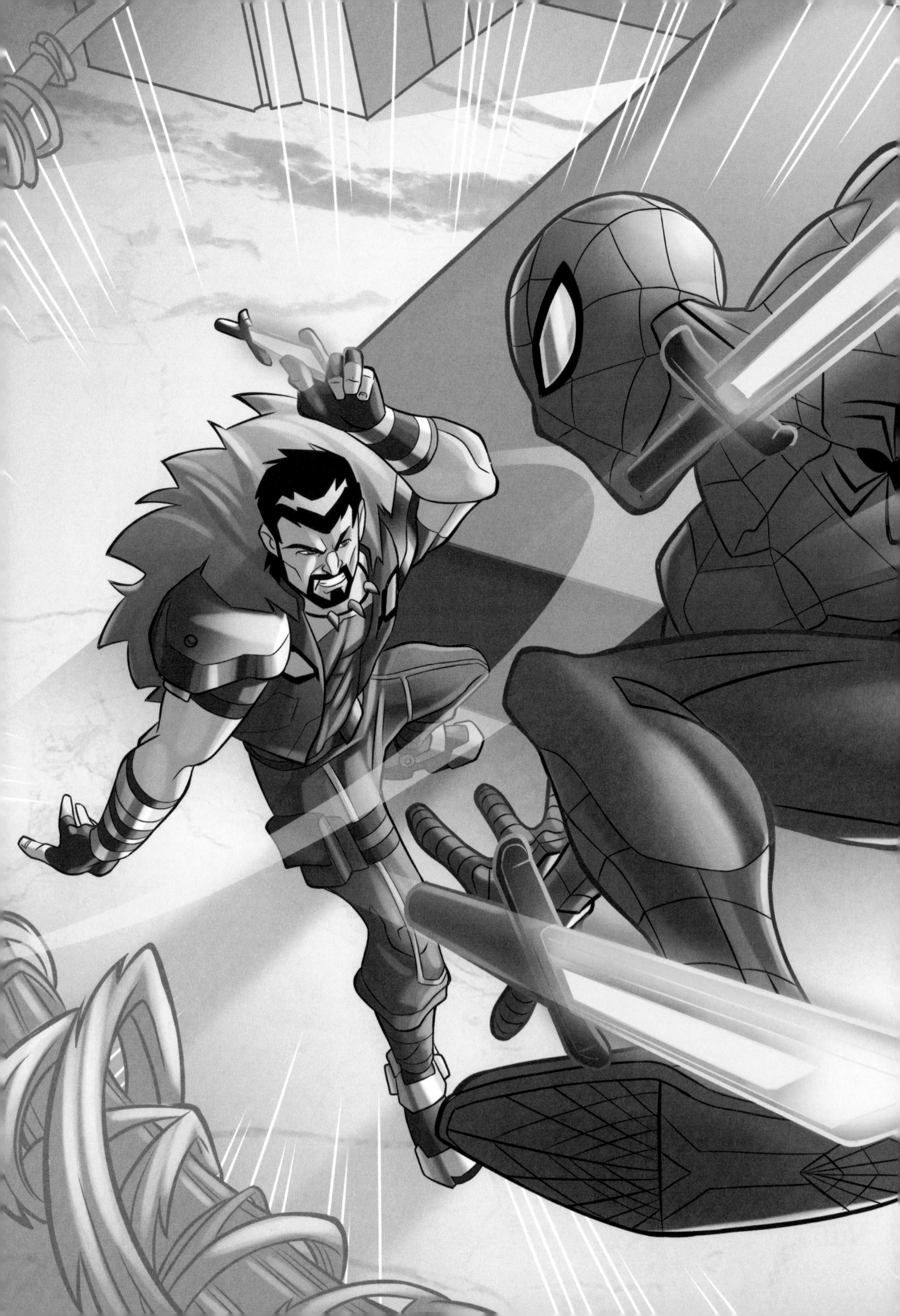

With the cheetahs under control, Spider-Man caught up
with the villainous hunter.

"You are nothing but a minor nuisance. I did not come
here for you, but if I must capture you, too, so be it!" Kraven
said. He began throwing knives at the web-slinging hero.
Unfortunately for Kraven, Spidey's trusty spider-sense made
it impossible for him to land an attack.

"What's the matter, Kraven?" Spider-Man asked. "Can't
catch a little spider?"

"Maybe it would help if you took care of that smell first, Kraven. P-U! Or do they not have showers in the jungle?" Spider-Man joked.

Blinded with anger, Kraven was unable to focus on the fight with the two Super Heroes. Spider-Man quickly used his web-shooters to disarm Kraven, giving Black Panther the perfect opening for an attack.

"Now you will pay for the crimes you have committed against the animal kingdom!" Black Panther added, before delivering the final blow to Kraven. The hunter was clearly no match for the strength and speed of the King of Wakanda.

Kraven was finally defeated.

"Beaten by a spider and a cat," Kraven mumbled.

"What's wrong? Don't like being held in captivity?" Spider-Man asked.

Black Panther addressed the crowd of frightened spectators. "You are all safe! These majestic creatures are not the enemy. They deserve respect and compassion. And thank you, Spider-Man, for helping me save them."

Spider-Man was caught off guard by the Black Panther's kind words. "Wow. Thanks, Black Panther. Now might not be a good time, but do you mind if we take a selfie?"

Seeing Spots

It was a wonderfully sunny day. Peter Parker and Gwen Stacy were strolling through Central Park, about to buy hot dogs from a vending cart. "Ketchup, mustard, and relish?" Peter asked.

"You know me too well, Parker," Gwen said, smiling.

Peter reached into his pocket to pay for the hot dogs when Gwen reached for her purse.

"My treat," she said.

Before Peter could argue, a strange black circle appeared below Gwen's purse. The friends were shocked when a white arm covered in black spots came shooting out of the hole. It grabbed Gwen's purse! Another circle appeared above them. Inside, a man's head appeared.

A menacing voice erupted from the circle. "What a lovely bag. I'm sorry, but I don't believe there will be any hot dogs today."

As suddenly as they appeared, the thief and his black circles disappeared. Gwen was shocked. Peter's eyes narrowed. He was not going to let some freaky villain ruin his perfect day with Gwen.

"Wait here!" Peter exclaimed. Before Gwen could say anything, Peter bolted out of sight.

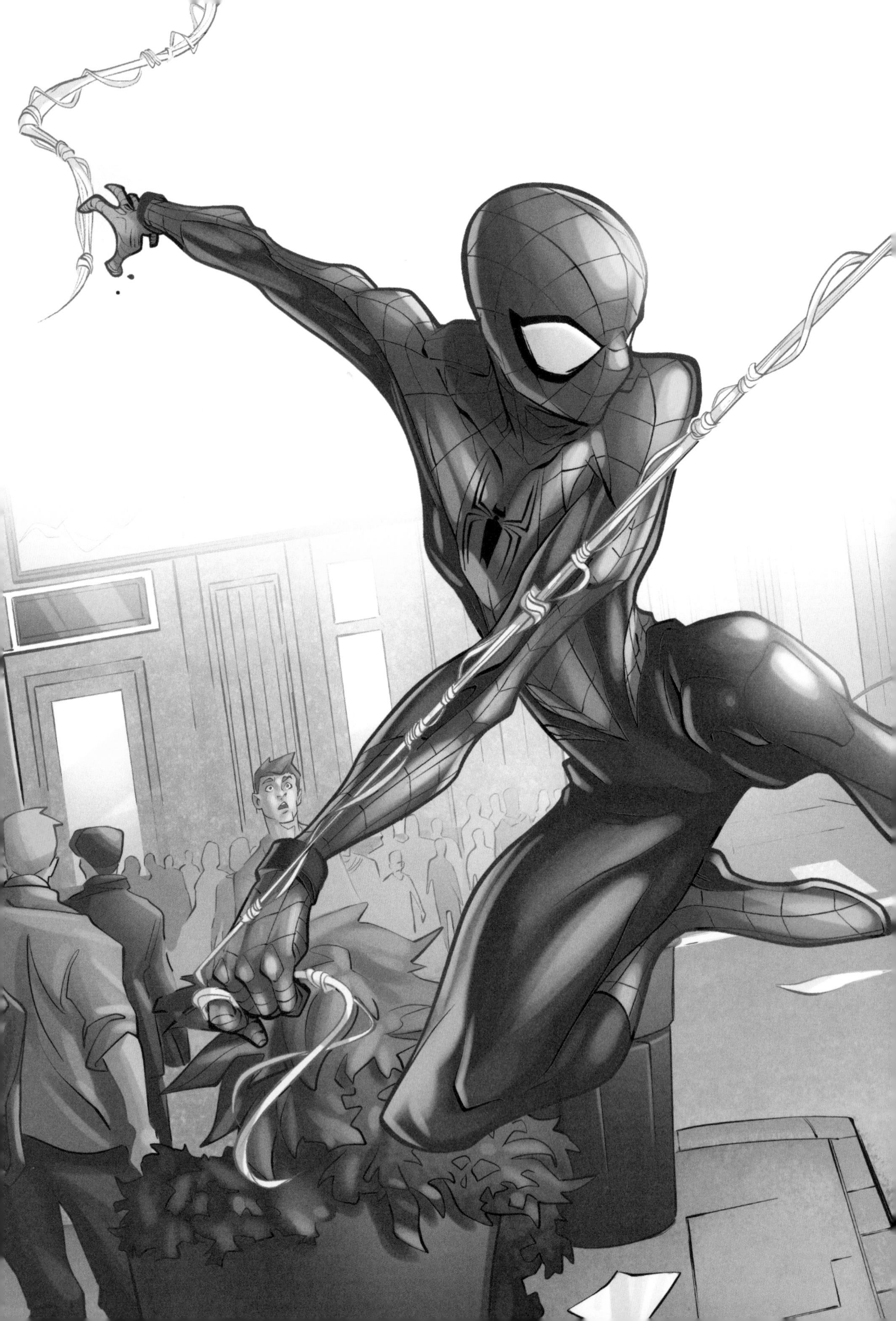

Peter ducked into an alley and changed into his Spider-Man suit to chase down the thief. He had been reading about this polka-dotted villain in the paper—a robber they called the Spot! Swinging high, Spider-Man looked out over the streets of New York for signs of the criminal.

"Ha! I *spot* you!" he chuckled as he saw black circles appear beside another potential victim. He swung off to face his foe.

Spider-Man managed to web the purse before the Spot could snatch it.

"I think you've collected enough for one day, Spot."

"Spider-Man! I've been waiting to run into you," the Spot said. "Over and over."

Suddenly, black circles appeared all around Spidey. Out of them came fists, hitting Spider-Man as the Spot appeared and reappeared in different directions. The villain was so fast that even Spider-Man's spider-sense couldn't keep up.

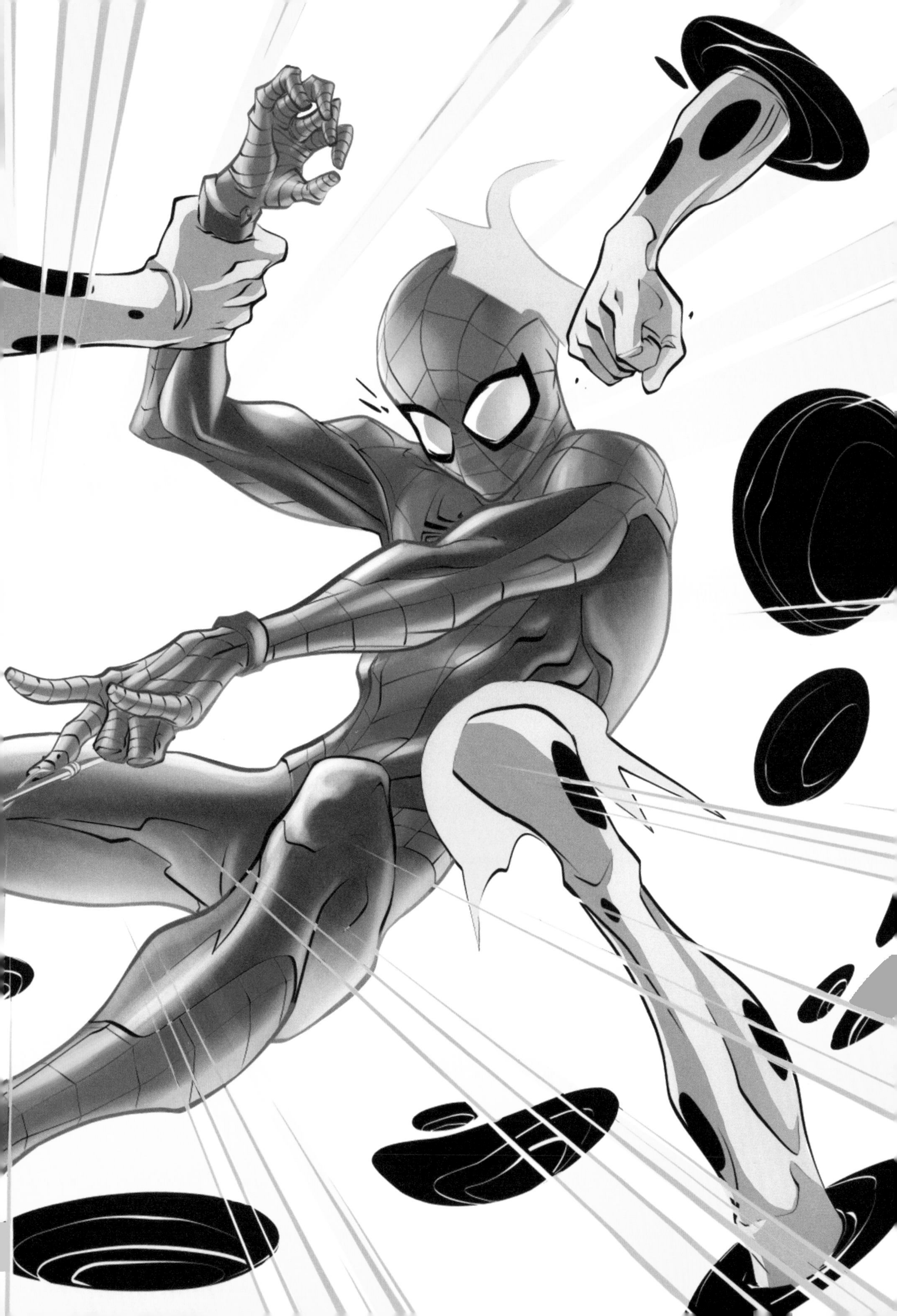

Spider-Man fell, beaten by the Spot. The teleporting villain appeared over him, laughing.

"Better luck next time, Bug-Brain!" the Spot taunted, vanishing into thin air.

Feeling woozy, Spidey realized he was going to need some help defeating this new menace. Fortunately, he knew just who to call.

Spidey swung to an abandoned church, hoping this was still the place his friends used as a hideout.

"If anyone can help me, it'll be these two," he muttered, knowing he was running out of options. The Spot was going to be hard to defeat.

Although they had only teamed up a few times before, and one of the two could be kind of creepy, Spider-Man knew he could trust this duo to help him get the job done.

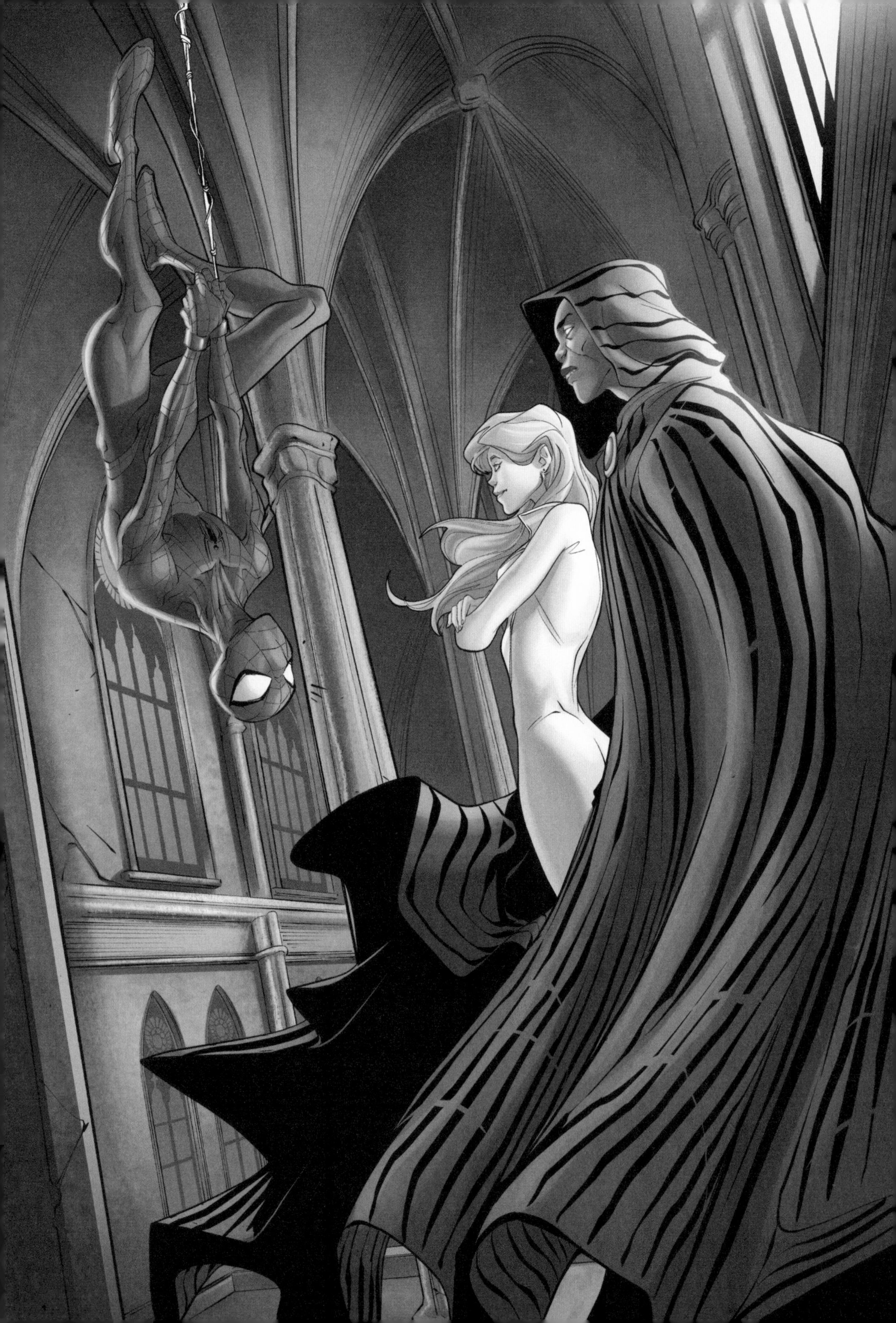

"Cloak! Dagger! Man, am I glad to see you guys," Spider-Man said as he entered the church. He quickly filled them in on his encounter with the Spot.

"I need your help." Spidey turned to Cloak. "I know you're used to popping in and out of thin air, too."

"I have felt someone tapping into my teleportation force recently," Cloak noted. "It seems this Spot and I share a connection through multiple dimensions."

That gave Dagger an idea. "If we can follow the energy Cloak is feeling, it could lead us to the Spot. Then my light daggers could help trap him there by draining his energy."

With the plan set, the heroes dove into the darkness of Cloak's cape, and disappeared.

When the trio reappeared,
they found themselves in the
Spot's secret hideout. It was
filled with all the stolen
purses, jewels, and other
items the thief had taken on
his crime spree.

"Spider-Man! How did you
find me here? And who are these
freaks?" the Spot asked, shocked.

Spider-Man just smiled.
"Looks like you're not the only
disappearing act in town, Spot."

The Spot tore the teleporting discs off of his suit, threw them around the room, and started to dive into them. He was ready to attack! But this time, the good guys were ready, too.

Bright knives shot out of Dagger's hands and burst into the dark circles. Her illuminating power filled the darkness in which the Spot thrived. They pushed out the Spot, cutting off his escape.

Spider-Man quickly webbed the villain before he could try his teleportation tricks again.

"Hmm, looks like you're stuck. I guess you could say my webs are *spot*-on!"

Dagger chuckled at Spider-Man's bad joke, while Cloak's icy stare never wavered.

Their plan worked! The Spot's thieving days were over.

The heroes helped return the stolen items. As the pile grew smaller, Spidey recognized one of the purses and grabbed it.

"Not enough pockets in your suit?" Dagger asked with a wink.

"Hey, bad jokes are my thing," Spider-Man replied.

Then with a quiet whoosh, Cloak whisked Dagger and the Spot away.

Back in Central Park, Peter Parker came running back to Gwen. There was a police officer handing over her purse.

"Gwen! You got it back!" Peter exclaimed.

"It was incredible, Peter! Spider-Man caught the thief and brought all the stolen items back. Including my purse."

Peter blushed. "Wow, he's a real hero."

"But you are just as brave, Peter," Gwen said, hugging her friend. "Thanks for looking out for me."

Peter grinned. "I'm sorry I couldn't do more."

"Well," Gwen said, handing the hot dog vendor money, "you certainly did enough to earn this hot dog. My treat, as promised."

"You're the best," Peter said as he chewed. "Wow, this really hits the *spot*."

The Amazing Incredible Spider-Hulk

Spider-Man and the Avengers were having dinner at a restaurant after they battled Ultron in Central Park. As the heroes ate, Iron Man challenged Hulk to an arm-wrestling contest. But Iron Man's armored gauntlets were no match for the Hulk.

"Hulk strong. Too easy," Hulk said.

Spider-Man was a little jealous of his big green pal. *I'm strong, but I'm not* Hulk *strong,* he thought. *If I could do everything the Hulk can do, I'd be the perfect Super Hero!*

Outside the restaurant, Spider-Man watched as a little girl shyly tugged at the Hulk's pant leg. "Excuse me," she mumbled. "Will you sign my autograph book?"

The green Avenger nodded graciously. But when he grabbed the pencil, he accidentally crushed it. Spidey could see that the Hulk was upset. He approached Hulk as the disappointed girl walked away.

"Hey, big guy, why the frown?" Spidey asked.

Spider-Man was surprised to hear that the Hulk sometimes wanted to be, as he put it, "more puny, like Bug-Man."

"Isn't that something," Spider-Man began. "I was just thinking about how sometimes I'd rather be more like you!" Just then, they received an important message from S.H.I.E.L.D. Nick Fury was unveiling an important new invention!

At S.H.I.E.L.D. headquarters, everyone saw Nick Fury standing next to a high-tech device capped by an enormous purple gemstone. Fury explained that they were there to witness a demonstration of a machine that would allow two Super Heroes to temporarily swap abilities. This way, they could catch Super Villains off guard.

Spidey and the Hulk couldn't believe what they were hearing. It would be like switching places! When Fury asked for volunteers, two hands immediately went up: a big green one and a smaller red one.

Spider-Man and the Hulk stood side by side over a big red *X* on the floor. Fury activated the device. The machine started to hum, and the purple gemstone glowed. It shot out a beam, covering both the Hulk and Spider-Man.

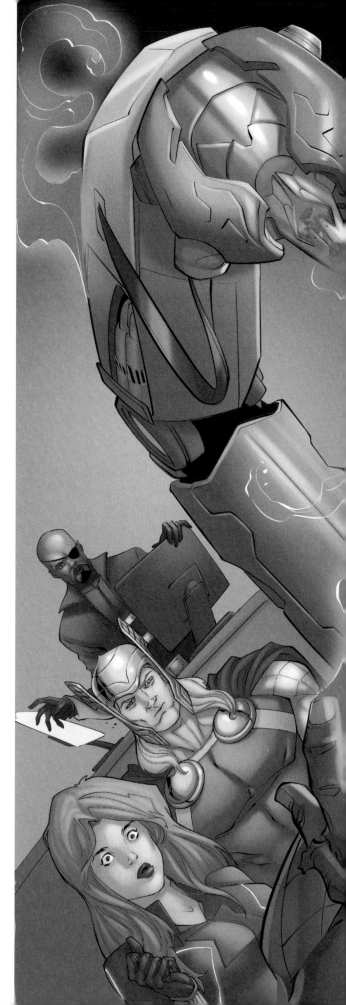

But the machine overheated, causing an explosion that shook the room! When the smoke cleared, everyone stared at the figure standing on the red *X*. It wasn't Spidey. It wasn't the Hulk. It looked like both of them . . . combined! Two heroes had merged into one hybrid creature— the Spider-Hulk!

Peering at Iron Man's armor, Spider-Hulk studied his reflection in its gleaming surface. The face that stared back at him was familiar, and yet . . . unfamiliar. Confused and frustrated, Spider-Hulk couldn't control his feelings. "Bug-Hulk SMASH!" he yelled, pounding his fists into the floor.

Captain America tried to calm down the heroic hybrid. "At ease, soldier!" Cap shouted over the noise. But before he could continue, Spider-Hulk grabbed Cap's shield and flung it into the wall. Then, the frightened Spider-Hulk turned and crashed through the glass window. The Avengers raced after him.

Spider-Hulk couldn't think clearly. It felt as though there were two separate voices in his head! He just wanted to get away from the people trying to capture him. He didn't realize his pursuers were his friends, the Avengers. "Bug-Hulk's bug-sense tingling," he muttered to himself.

Spider-Hulk tried using his webbing to outrun the Avengers, but when he attempted to swing away, his body twisted awkwardly in the air. The web-line snapped, and Spider-Hulk fell, smashing into the pavement below!

With Spider-Hulk momentarily weakened, Hawkeye quickly came up with a plan. He had sometimes calmed the Hulk down with a nursery rhyme, so he sat down and began reading to Spider-Hulk. It worked too well. The hybrid hero thought it was bedtime, and he fled looking for a midnight snack!

This gave Black Widow an idea. The Avengers would draw Spider-Hulk back to S.H.I.E.L.D. headquarters using the one thing both Spider-Man and the Hulk love: food! When Thor and Black Widow found Spider-Hulk, he was ransacking every hot dog cart in the city looking for snacks. Thor stood in his path and tried to lure Spider-Hulk away with a delicious chocolate cake from the bakery.

But before Thor could lead the way back to headquarters, Spider-Hulk swallowed the entire cake. The new Super Hero also had a super appetite!

Iron Man knew that Spider-Man was really Peter Parker, a teenager who couldn't resist his Aunt May's famous wheat cakes. So the armored Avenger instructed his personal chef to make enough wheat cakes to feed a small country. In other words, enough wheat cakes to feed one Spider-Hulk.

Iron Man zoomed around the city, leaving a trail of wheat cakes for his fused friend to follow. It worked! The Spider-Hulk gobbled each tasty treat, leading him closer and closer to the device that caused all this chaos in the first place!

Spider-Hulk was so busy wolfing down wheat cakes that he didn't notice he was sitting on the big red *X*. He swallowed the last piece of wheat cake and said, "Spider-Hulk wants maple—" But before he could finish his sentence, Nick Fury pressed the reverse button. Once again the purple gemstone glowed and Spider-Hulk was shot with an energy beam.

When the light faded, two heroes stepped forth: Spider-Man and the Hulk!

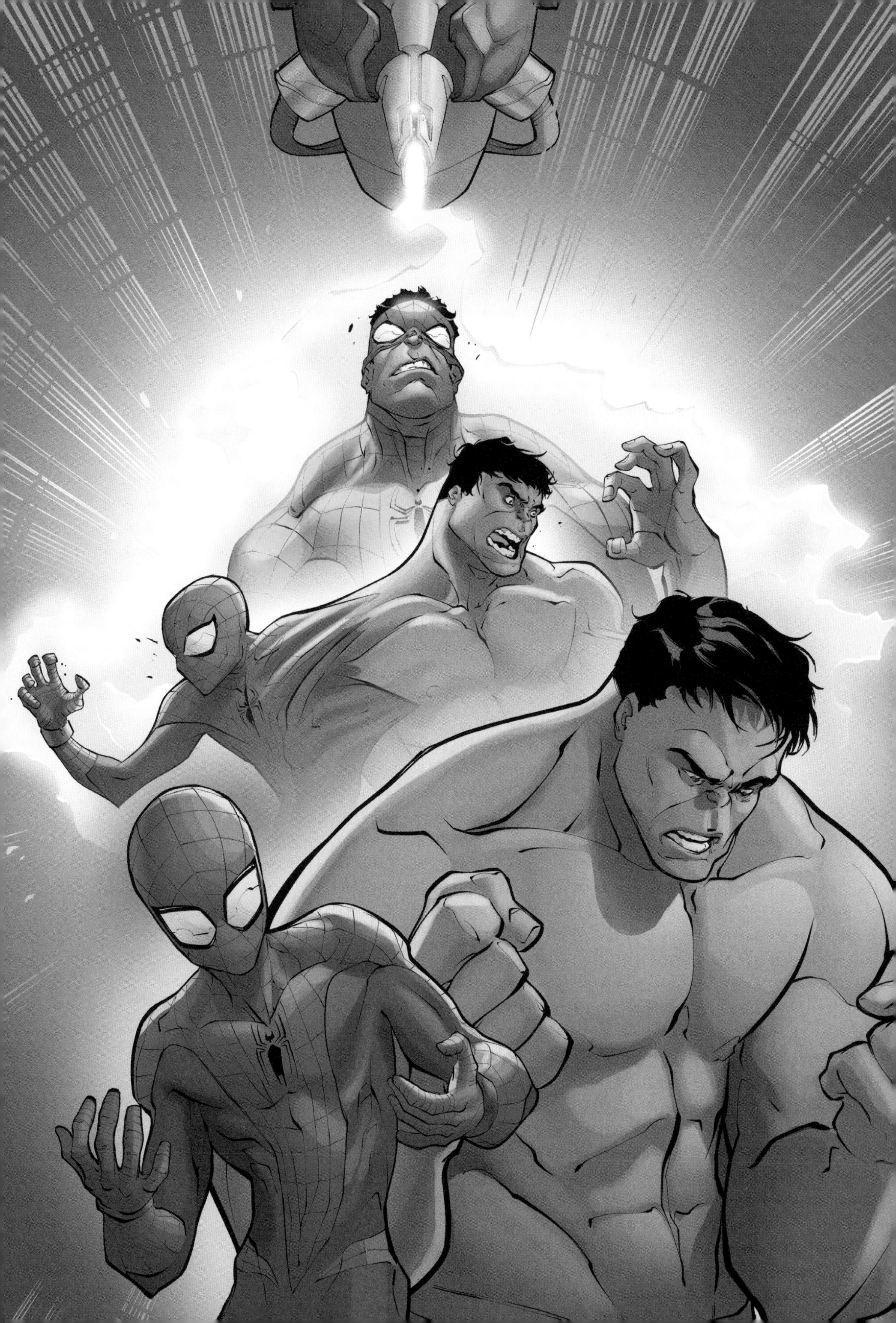

"I really learned something today," Spider-Man told the Hulk. "I used to think I wanted to be more like you. But being Spider-Hulk just . . . didn't feel like me. And I like being me."

The green goliath nodded. "Hulk learned something, too," he began. "Hulk learned that Bug-Man's puny costume is bad fit on Hulk-size body!" The two friends laughed. Then they patted their bellies and turned to the other Avengers. "Okay," Spider-Man said with a wink, "who's up for some dessert?"

Mega Meltdown

New York City was in the middle of a heat wave. Unfortunately for Spider-Man, that wasn't going to stop the city's criminals.

"Seriously, guys? Committing crimes in a city full of Super Heroes? Not a great idea," Spider-Man said to the two bank robbers he had just webbed.

Despite the heat, Spider-Man noticed that the criminals were shivering.

"If we're going to be stuck here, how about some more webbing, huh?"

Why were those guys acting like it's cold out? Spider-Man thought as he swung away. *It's been a scorcher for weeks!*

As he swung closer to Times Square, Spider-Man's spider-sense began to tingle. The wind started to whip around him as the temperature steadily dropped. *Maybe it is a little chilly today.*

Just then, Spider-Man came across the source of the changing weather. A gigantic portal had opened up in the sky, sending snow flurries down upon the city. Loki, the trickster god of Asgard, was standing atop a skyscraper clutching a Cosmic Cube!

Spider-Man swung down to confront the Super Villain. "Ah, the Spider. I invite you to witness the start of my glorious reign," Loki said proudly. "With Earth destroyed, those pesky Avengers will finally be out of my way."

"Yeah, right," Spider-Man said. "What are a few snowflakes going to do?"

"Just wait until you meet my friends," Loki cackled. The ground began to rumble as Loki lifted up the Cosmic Cube. Suddenly, a group of Frost Giants leaped from the portal right in the middle of Times Square! Parked cars were crushed under the weight of the massive giants as they lumbered through the streets. The frightened tourists ran for cover as sparks from collapsing billboards rained down upon the chaotic scene.

"Meet the Frost Giants of Jotunheim," Loki said in an otherworldly voice. "Now that I have the Cosmic Cube, they are under my control!" Spider-Man knew there was only one thing to do. He leaped into action.

Thwip! Spidey shot his webs through the air. He sailed over Times Square, straight toward one of the giants.

"Hey, Snowball! Over here!" Spider-Man shouted.

As he got closer to the giants, he narrowly missed a massive club swinging toward him.

"What do I look like—some kind of bug?" he said.

Spider-Man looked down at his suit.

". . . Oh, yeah, well, I can't really blame you."

Spider-Man swung out of reach, then approached the Frost Giants once more. The mindless giants paid him no attention. They were only concerned with one thing: destruction.

I don't have enough webbing left to tie up Frosty and friends, Spidey thought. *But this should slow them down.*

Spider-Man fired a web across the street. He hoped this barrier would stop the Frost Giants' march.

It looked like the Frost Giants were finally going to be stopped when . . . BOOM!

Spider-Man was shocked to witness the Frost Giants step on his web barrier, causing two billboards to crash to the ground.

Just then, Spider-Man spotted an Avengers Quinjet flying over.

"It's about time!" Spidey exclaimed. He knew that with friends like Captain America, Thor, Black Widow, and Iron Man on his side, Loki and his snow buddies didn't stand a chance!

Spider-Man approached the jet as it landed on a nearby rooftop. As the cargo ramp lowered, Spider-Man saw only one hero. One very small hero.

"So, what's the situation here?"

167

"Ant-Man?!" Spider-Man was shocked as the miniature hero walked down the ramp. "Where's everyone else?"

"The Avengers are busy with Thanos," Ant-Man said. "That guy never takes a day off. Nick Fury called and said there was some trouble in the city. I'm here to back you up, pal."

"No offense, but I was expecting some bigger guns," Spider-Man said. "How are two bugs going to stop three giants?"

"Well, looks like these 'two bugs' are all New York has today."

Spider-Man knew Ant-Man was right. Two heads were better than one. And with that, Ant-Man grabbed on to Spidey's suit as he swung back toward the wintry chaos.

As soon as Spider-Man and
Ant-Man rejoined the Frost Giants,
one of them threw a car at the two heroes.

"Look out!" Ant-Man exclaimed.

"Way ahead of you!" Spider-Man responded as he
swiftly dodged the car. "But this heavy snowfall isn't making
anything easier! Any ideas?"

"Well, if they want to head to Central Park, I can send in
some ants to ruin their picnic," Ant-Man said sarcastically.

"Even so, it's not warm enough for a picnic," Spider-Man said. "But wait! That gives me an idea! How much do you know about electricity?"

"More than you, kid," Ant-Man said. "And I think I know where you're going with this."

Evading attacks from Loki's Frost Giants, Spidey swung toward Times Tower, the brightest building in the city.

As Spider-Man approached the tower, Ant-Man was able to jump just before a Frost Giant grabbed Spider-Man's webbing. The giant pulled the webs, yanking him off of the tower.

"Oomph!" Spider-Man exclaimed as he crashed onto the hard cement.

Ant-Man knew Spider-Man couldn't hold back the giants for long. He squeezed between the bright billboards. Once inside, the small hero was able to hack into the main power grid.

"Hey, you big bullies!" Ant-Man shouted. "How about turning up the heat!"

Suddenly, Times Square began to brighten. The lights became brighter and brighter until the light from the billboards was blinding. Hit with 161 megawatts of power, the Frost Giants quickly began to shrink until they vanished completely.

"It's working!" Spider-Man said as he swung to face Loki. "Looks like your Frost Giants should've brought some sunscreen."

"Spider-Man!" Loki roared. "You did this?"

Spider-Man quickly shot a web straight toward Loki. "I had some help. Not too bad for a couple of bugs, huh?"

With Loki blinded by webbing, Spider-Man was able to take the Cosmic Cube out of his grasp. Using the power of the Cosmic Cube, Spider-Man opened up a portal and sent Loki back to Jotunheim.

"I'll be back, Spider—I always come back!" Loki screamed as he was pulled into the portal at high speed.

"Defeated Loki, melted a bunch of Frost Giants, and caused a blackout in Times Square," Ant-Man said. "Man, we deserve a vacation."

"You're right," Spider-Man responded. "But we still have to return this cube and restore power to Times Square."

"Yeah, but first . . . Spider! My ants and I challenge thee to a snowball fight!" Ant-Man said, mocking Loki.

"You're on!"

Attack of the Portal Crashers

BOOM! A tremendous noise echoed through the streets of New York City. The ground shook so hard that car alarms went off and stray cats hid under Dumpsters.

Spider-Man looked down, his spider-sense on high alert. He immediately spotted Iron Man fighting a strange feathery villain. It was Spider-Man's old enemy—the Vulture!

Spider-Man swooped in to help.

Working together, Spider-Man and Iron Man had the Vulture beat in no time.

"Thanks, kid," Iron Man said. "We make a pretty great team."

"You're welcome, Mr. Stark," Spider-Man said, blushing under his mask. Iron Man, billionaire Tony Stark, was a big deal.

"Please, Mr. Stark was my father," Iron Man joked. He put his arm around Spidey. "You know, some of the greatest victories have been won by heroes working as a team. Like the time Cap, Falcon, and I teamed up to fight Hydra, or when Widow and Hawkeye took down A.I.M. Cloak and Dagger are always helping Doctor Strange fight Dormammu. Every hero has certain strengths and weaknesses."

"Well, I usually work alone," Spider-Man explained. "I don't think I've earned my place among the real heroes yet."

"There's no shame in needing a little help," Iron Man said with a smile. "See ya around, kid."

As Iron Man rocketed away, Spider-Man began to think about how cool all the other heroes were, and how badly he wanted to prove himself. That gave him an idea. What if he threw a party for them? They deserved it—they saved the world every day, after all.

That night, Spider-Man went home and took off his suit. At home, he could be just regular old Peter Parker. The more Peter thought about it, the better he liked the idea of throwing a party for the other heroes. *A great party would definitely impress the Avengers!* he thought.

Peter immediately got to work. He wrote invitations to all the Super Heroes he could think of. He knew Central Park would be the perfect place to host the party. He'd bake a cake and maybe even make a piñata. It was going to be awesome!

Peter's invitations made their way to every
famous Super Hero in the world.

But one invitation made its way—entirely by
accident—through a rogue wormhole right into
the hands of Thanos, the cosmic Super Villain.

"All of Earth's Mightiest Heroes in one place?"
Thanos said, reading the invitation. "This is my
chance to destroy them all in one blow!"

The party started out great. Peter served delicious cupcakes and even made a Mysterio-shaped piñata. Everyone showed up and brought things for the party! Hulk had baked a green cake. Doctor Strange put on a dazzling light show. Hawkeye set up an indestructible game of whack-a-mole, and laughed as a frustrated Thor whacked away at it with his hammer. Captain America and Black Widow were playing Frisbee with Cap's shield, and Black Panther was beating Ant-Man at the pin-the-staff-on-the-Loki game. Everyone was having a great time!

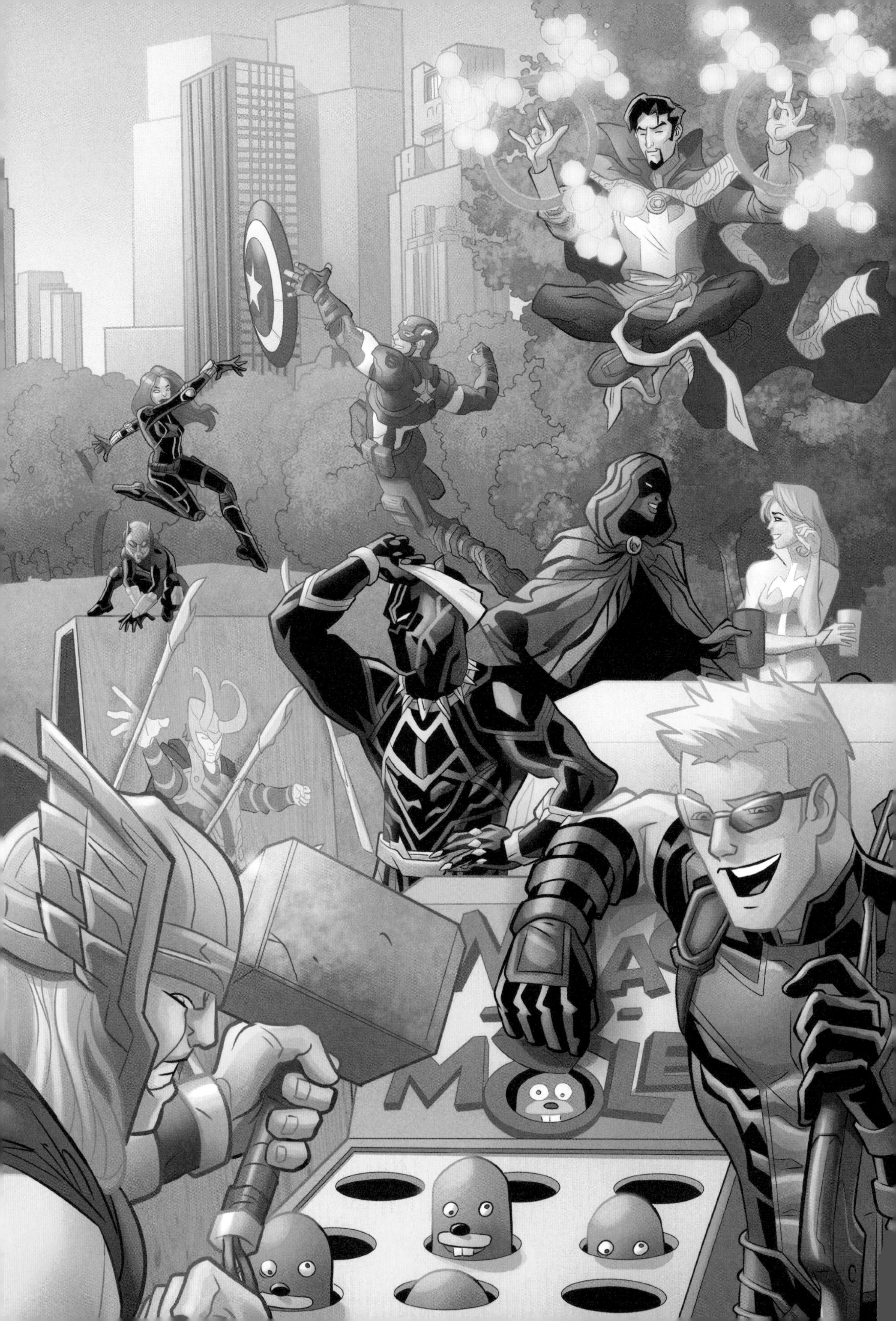
MOLE

Suddenly, the sky turned dark and stormy. Lightning cracked against the gray clouds. "We're under attack!" Captain America shouted as thousands of alien cyborgs started raining down on Central Park.

"It's the Chitauri!" Black Widow yelled.

Every hero leaped into action.

The scene fell into chaos as the world's greatest heroes battled the galaxy's fiercest enemy. With a *zap* of her electrostatic cuffs, Black Widow took out several cyborgs while Thor *plowed* through another dozen with his hammer. Iron Man and Captain America *blasted* Chitauri to pieces. Black Panther *slashed* at them with his vibranium claws. And as for Hulk . . . well, Hulk SMASHED.

Spider-Man watched in awe. Every hero was needed in this fight—and that included him! He threw himself into the battle, firing webs at lightning speed.

The greatest Super Heroes in the world, including Spider-Man, fought long and hard. Soon the tide of the battle was turning. Fallen cyborgs littered the ground.

But then, with a mighty CRACK, the sky split open and Thanos appeared. Spider-Man's heart sank. The Chitauri were bad news, but Thanos was way worse. The world was really in trouble now.

"I've got him!" cried Captain America. But Thanos saw Cap charging and threw him into a tree. Then Black Panther leaped at Thanos, kicking powerfully, but the blow bounced right off of Thanos's chest. Doctor Strange's magic couldn't contain the massive villain, and even Hawkeye's sharpest arrow bounced harmlessly away. One by one, the heroes were defeated.

Then Spider-Man remembered what Iron Man had told him: *Some of the greatest victories have been won by heroes working as a team.*

That's what they needed! None of them could defeat Thanos alone. But if they teamed up . . .

"Everybody!" Spider-Man cried. "We need to work together!"

With Spider-Man leading the assault, the heroes all fell in. Each hero brought their greatest strengths to the fight.

"We need to reverse the portal," Spider-Man realized. "Come on, heroes, let's knock this tough Titan into oblivion!" When the Super Heroes worked as one, they were an invincible army!

In the fiercest battle Central Park had ever seen, Spider-Man and his heroic friends banished Thanos to a far-off dimension in the multiverse. The world was safe.

"Teaching me my own words of wisdom?" Iron Man asked, slinging a metal-clad arm around Spider-Man's shoulders. "You're a pretty smart kid."

"Yeah, maybe even smarter than you." Spider-Man smiled.

"Hey, now, don't get crazy," Iron Man replied.

Spider-Man had finally won his place among the greatest heroes of the age, but it wasn't on his own. Spider-Man teamed up and saved the world!